MW00780686

Satan's Stone

The fourth book in the best selling
Demon Kissed Series

www.DemonKissed.com

Join over 43,000 fans on facebook!
www.facebook.com/DemonKissed

SATAN'S STONE

H.M. WARD

Laree Bailey Press

Laree Bailey Press, 4431 Loop 322, Abilene, TX 79602

Printed in the United States of America
First Printing: January 2012
10 9 8 7 6 5 4 3 2 1

Library of Congress Cataloging-in-Publication Data

Ward, H.M.
Torn / H.M. Ward – 1st ed.
 p. cm.
ISBN 978-0615584010

Other Books By H.M. Ward

DEMON KISSED

CURSED

TORN

SATAN'S STONE

THE 13TH PROPHECY

VALEFAR VOL. 1

BANE-VAMPIRE APOCALYPSE

Writing Satan's Stone has been truly amazing!
Thank you to the awesome fans who loved
Demon Kissed from the very beginning.

Demon Kissed

H.M. WARD

PAINTING OF IVY TAYLOR

SATAN'S STONE

CHAPTER ONE

The weapon was gripped tightly in my fist, hanging by my side. The silvery lethal tines were extended. Moving forward, I took another step down the dark hall. Ornate frames lined the walls and housed massive paintings. Paintings of rich tones and vivid scenes that came from the mind of someone long dead. The rug slid silently under my foot making it easier to move through the house unnoticed. There wasn't a person in sight. The house had a creepy quietness that seemed unnatural for a home this large. There should have been a housekeeper moving about the property. The kitchen should have been filled with the clatter of cooking, and the scent of coffee. But there was nothing.

Only silence.

This was the house. I was certain. The ornate banister was the same. The grand room below was identical. Intricate carvings lined the support beams of the second floor with leaves and ornate swirls—just like before. The dark wood gleamed just as it had the last time I was here. There wasn't a speck of dust anywhere, despite the fact that the home appeared abandoned. But I knew it wasn't. I knew he'd come back here. There were very few places to hide.

Finding the house again wasn't an issue, but getting there was another matter. Not being able to effonate without freeing the venom in my chest was… irritating. The night he slayed Al, the night she fell—was horror beyond words. My grip on my weapon tightened just thinking about it. I couldn't find Eric fast enough. Revenge lined the thoughts of my mind until it was overflowing. It'd taken too long to get here. He could be anywhere by now, but I suspected he was here. Old habits die hard and this place was a little too clean for an abandoned mansion.

Anger burned deep within me. I could hear it crackling in my ears like water in a greasy skillet. It surged into every last inch of my body. My muscles twitched, ready to fight. I wanted to fight. I wanted to kill Eric for what he did. I pushed the thoughts down, and took a steadying breath. If I failed to control my emotions, then my hair would turn into a purple torch. That would be counterproductive, since I didn't want him to know that I was here. My bare toes pressed against the floor. I took another step.

In front of me—at the end of the hall—were several doors. They stood in the darkness, large and imposing. A muted voice poured through the thick wood. The familiar inflections made a grin stretch across my lips. He was here. It was Eric's rich voice wafting through the darkness. His words weren't clear, but that didn't matter. I wasn't here to chat. And I didn't care who he was talking to.

Only one thought lingered in my mind—vengeance. Squeezing the grip on my weapon, I slid forward. As I looked down at the gleaming silver in my hand a strange sensation slithered up my spine. Twisting my wrist, I examined the blades. They curved like the claws of a massive animal. They were light like the sickle of a reaper. And in a matter of moments they would sink into Eric's flesh. He would fall to the floor and the blood that he used against me—the blood that I still yearned for—would drain from his body. A perverse sense of satisfaction flared within me, and twisted the smile tighter on my lips.

My eyes shifted back to the door. Light spilled under the dark slab of wood, forming a golden puddle of light on the carpet. Extending my hand forward, I reached for the golden knob. The metal scraped lightly as the knob twisted in my hand. The tiny sound made my heart lurch in my chest. My breath caught in my throat. Swallowing hard, I held the twisted knob in my sweaty hand, afraid to allow it to twist back. Eric kept talking on the other side of the door. If he noticed the sound, he had chosen to ignore it. Forcing my wildly beating heart to steady, I placed my palm on the dark wooden door and gently pushed the door open a little bit—so I could see what was happening. If he saw me, I'd have to attack. The element of surprise would be lost. But he was speaking with someone, and I couldn't throw myself in front of them without knowing who it was. As the door cracked opened, I could barely breathe. I held it steady, still refusing to release the knob.

My eyes rimmed violet. Heat washed through me as anger pressed to flow into the rest of my body, but I repressed it. It wasn't time yet. Pushing the foaming rage back down was like trying to subdue a rabid dog with a pat on the head. Pain twisted inside my stomach when longing and vengeance crashed together.

That's when I saw him.

H.M. Ward

CHAPTER TWO

Eric was standing with his back to me. His arms were folded confidently across his chest. A dark shirt clung to his torso. Jeans hugged his narrow hips. Golden brown hair was tousled and gleaming in the early morning sunlight. A massive window was behind him, painting him in rays of light. When I saw him, a wave of lust washed over me. Desire pulsed, warming my body. My heart throbbed in my chest. My eyes slid over his slender frame causing my fingers to twitch. I wanted to undress him, button by button. The thought of feeling his skin beneath my hands coursed through me. My lips parted, and a shallow breath rushed out. My eyes slipped over his entire body in a gaze that would have made me blush. I leaned harder on the door, fighting the lust that hazed my thoughts.

The blood lust was an issue, but I'd overcome it before. I thought I could do it again, but I didn't plan on spying on him before attacking. The delay sent my body into an internal war. I fought back, trying to subdue the effect of his blood on me. In the end my mind made a merger that the lust-driven side and the vengeful side could agree on—blood. They both wanted his blood spilled on the floor, taken from his body so that he was no more.

Eric didn't move as I drooled at him behind his back. He seemed unaware of my presence. And no one was with him. He appeared to be speaking into a phone on the desk. Hope swelled within me. This is what I'd wanted. The muscles in my arms twitched, making my fingers press against the blade in my hand. The haze of lust that had glued me to the door was thick. I had to temper it, and I knew exactly how.

Since the night Al died, I'd pressed back the anger and grief at her loss. The feelings didn't stop, but I couldn't deal with them until Eric was dead. So, I shoved them deep inside of me. Anger, betrayal, lust, remorse, and more—they all lingered in the back of my mind, silently choking me for weeks. But now, now they would fuel my vengeance. They would topple the effects of Eric's blood. There was only one chance, and

I knew it. Eric was a better fighter than me, and he wasn't wounded. I was. There was one chance to kill him, and I took it.

The floodgates of my mind—the ones that held my rage in check—cracked opened. I felt a wave of raw emotions rip through my body. Any trace of lust drowned in a wave of blind hatred. Every part of me tingled, and tensed as I threw my shoulder into the door. It flew open, crashing against the wall with a loud thud. And I sprang at him. My body flew through the air with my hair streaming wildly behind me, illuminated with a faint purple flame at the tips. A singed scent filled my nostrils. I disregarded it. The muscles in my back flexed. The power built in my arms. And I swung my deadly silver blades at Eric's chest.

But, Eric didn't turn. He didn't move. Instead, he continued to stare out the window as I hurtled through the air toward him. Something was wrong. A desperate cry ripped out of my throat as I tried to stop myself, but it was too late. I collided with the stone-still Eric, knocking him to the floor. As soon as my fingers touched his cold arm, the boy turned to ash. Springing to my feet, I whipped my head around the room. No one else was there. My heart hammered in my chest. Sweat poured down my spine. I spun around looking for him, my eyes sifting through shadows. I stepped away from the pile of ash, and spoke into the empty room.

CHAPTER THREE

"I know you're here," I growled. "I can smell your blood through the darkness. This thing wasn't you." I pointed at the pile of ash. "Masking yourself won't save you—not from me." Narrowing my eyes, I turned slowly allowing my senses to take over. Keeping my weapon ready, I moved slowly toward one of the corners in the room. Heavy drapes hung from the ceiling to the floor, preventing the morning sun from illuminating this area—but I could see through the darkness. That wasn't what drew my attention. It was a small detail, a detail that might have been overlooked by someone else. The light that spilled across the floor from the other window came to a certain point and abruptly stopped, as if something were blocking it. As if something were standing there.

Without hesitation, I launched myself at the spot. I flew through the air, ready to strike. Eric's golden eyes appeared in front of me. Before I could move his arm shot out, reaching for my neck. I was jerked to a stop as his fingers closed around my throat. My toes scraped against the ground as Eric dragged me toward him. His arms flexed and lifted me to his face. Our eyes met. The lust that was stirring within me exploded. It felt more powerful. More seductive. Eric's touch filled me with desire. It didn't matter that he was strangling me. I wanted him. I needed him. Suddenly, every bit of tension that laced through my body evaporated, and I relaxed in his grip.

Eric's hand tightened around my throat. He dragged me closer to his face, so close our noses were touching. His soft pink lips were perfect. I wanted to taste them. Eric laughed. "After all this time, and you finally found me… It's been, what? Three weeks or so?" His lips twisted into a smile. I was transfixed by his voice, his words, and his scent—but something inside of me was crying out with rage too intense to ignore. It made me feel completely insane. My body didn't know which impulses to follow—lust or rage.

Rage. Moving suddenly, I swung my blade at him. The long silver tines sank into his side forming four punctures in his flesh. Then I pulled. The silver sliced through his skin like a piece of tissue paper. I stared into his eyes as my weapon slid across his gut, spilling Eric's blood. Blood I wanted. Blood I needed. His grip on my throat loosened, as his side ripped open. But he didn't release me. That much of Eric's blood was irresistible. But as soon as the scent intensified, so did my fury. The muscles in my arms flexed, and I twisted the blade in my hand, ready to shove it upward to Eric's heart.

Eric looked down at me, golden eyes calculating. He didn't seem surprised by my attack. His expression was that of annoyance, but when my blade turned upward, he moved faster than me. His free hand wrapped around the blade of my weapon. The hissing sound of his sizzling flesh filled my ears, as he tried to jerk it away from me. But I refused to release the weapon. As he twisted, so did I, but his grip on my neck held me in place. The lust burning through my body made me weak. Eric pulled, again. I tightened my grip, but my fingers slipped over the hilt with the sharp tug. The deadly tines cut deeply into my palm. They nearly severed my fingers from my hand as the weapon was jerked away from me. Slick warmth quickly turned to fire, as blood flowed from the wounds. Eric's sharp tug made the blade cut into his fingers, as well. When my grip slackened, he yanked and pitched the weapon across the room. The comb clattered across the floor leaving a streak of blood. Eric looked at me from under his brow, wiping his burnt hand on his jeans.

His fingers were still tight around my throat when he jerked me toward his face, "You're a fool." His gold eyes bore into me, never wavering.

A smile twisted my lips, as my good hand pulled on Eric's death-grip on my throat. My body shifted slightly. I could breathe. Inhaling only made my head spin harder. There was so much blood. I could barely think. But there was a desire, lingering in the back of my mind. I did what it wanted—I clenched my injured hand closed, feeling pain shoot up my arm. But I didn't care. Blood wrapped around my wrist, flowing down to my elbow, and dripped onto the floor. Eric's expression shifted, and he opened his mouth to speak. Before he uttered a single word, I lunged my bleeding fist forward. My hand flew at his mouth. Blood dripped from the wound, covering every inch of my fist. My fingers flattened at the last second. And I pushed my fingers past Eric's lips and into his mouth. His tongue flicked against the intrusion and he tried to close his mouth, but it was too late. His hand released my neck as both arms shot up to push my bloody hand away, but I felt it. He swallowed. My blood slid down his throat. That was all I needed.

I fell to the floor laughing, leaving a smear of blood across the silken carpet. I cradled my bloody hand to my chest and looked up at him, utterly cocky. "You should have killed me when you had the chance." I slid my feet under me, and pushed myself off the floor. Walking over to him slowly, I saw the look of horror on his face. A smile slid across my lips.

The expression on Eric's face shifted. It became more intense—more focused. He stalked towards me, one step at a time. His mouth pulled back into a wicked smile. His tongue slid over the blood that stained his lips, like he couldn't get enough. It was what I wanted. I wanted him to swallow my blood. I wanted control over him, so I could kill him. But instead of being elated, fear coursed through me. The look on Eric's face was predatory. My foot slid backwards as he neared me. Eric was breathing hard. Dried blood clung to his shirt where the wound I'd inflicted on his flank was already healing. Saliva filled my mouth as my eyes slid over his side, forcing me to swallow. Eric leaned close to my face and looked down at me. Fear coursed through me. My gaze shot across the room to my weapon. It was out of reach.

His voice was seduction, "Ivy." My stomach floated inside of me as he spoke. I couldn't move. Heart racing, I looked up at him, breathing hard through my mouth. Eric reached for my wounded hand. It was cradled against my chest. Crimson ribbons of blood were still wrapping around my wrist, and sliding down my arm. The wound hadn't healed yet. I watched as he reached for me. His fingers grazed my breast, as he slid his hand under mine, and lifted it to his mouth.

Eric's gaze locked with mine. He pressed a kiss into my palm, before licking the pooled blood at the center. My heart raced as I watched him, mesmerized. The trance continued, as he pressed my hand to his lips and kissed it softly. His tongue slid across my wrist, and licked away the blood that had streaked across my pale skin. Unable to speak, I stared at him. His actions were carnal. It didn't shame him. It didn't even make him pause. He saw what he wanted and took it.

Al.

That was what he did with Al. He saw what he wanted, and he took it. With a snap I came back to myself. My mind cut through the lust induced haze. I jerked my wrist away from him. Eric laughed softly as I tore my hand out of his grip. Surprised and suspicious, I looked up at him. I didn't remember laughing like that when he fed me his blood. Eric's blood was so powerful that I could barely think when he first gave it to me.

But Eric smiled at me, alert and unhindered. "Did you really think that would work?" He turned and picked up my blade. The weapon hissed in his hand. Eric tossed it to me. The silver blades flashed in the sunlight as it flew toward me. I reached up and snatched it out of the air. Dread started to pool in my stomach as he moved across the room. The confident stance of his shoulders didn't waiver.

"Yes." My eyes were wide. "It should have…" My voice was deep. I tried to keep it from shaking. I wrapped my fingers tighter around my weapon, but it was my left hand. And I wasn't a lefty. My right hand was still healing and unable to grasp the hilt. The wound was deep, and cut into the bone. Wounds like that took more time to heal. Time I didn't have.

Eric turned with a smug smile on his face. "But it didn't… You don't have enough demon blood. You're not a Valefar." He turned and walked toward me, his eyes sliding over the curves of my body as he moved. I swallowed hard, trying to fight off the haze of lust that froze me to the floor. He lifted his hand and took a stray curl between his fingers. I released a breath. He looked me in the eye, "You don't have enough demon blood to make me crave your blood. You can't bind me—it's too late. And you cannot kill me," he paused, dropping the lock of hair, and looked down into my face. His eyes searched mine, as if they revealed something hidden. When his lips parted again, a thin smile line spread across his mouth, and he said,

"Because you need me. You want me." He slid his hands around me waist and jerked me towards him.

I gasped, as he cradled me tightly in his arms. I wanted to fight back, but it was like I was drugged. Eric's touch shattered my thoughts, breaking them into a million incomprehensible pieces. He pressed his body to mine and tucked his finger under my chin. When he pulled my face up to look into his, he said, "We are the same, you and I."

His touch melted my mind. I wanted it. I wanted him. To feel his rough hands slide across my skin… My lashes lowered as I realized what I was thinking. As I realized he was right. Eric's golden gaze was intense. He lowered his face toward me. His smooth lips were so close that I shuddered. Warm breath washed across my face, as Eric's fingers tangled in my hair. His other hand slid down my shoulder, gently caressing my breast, before it landed on my waist. I gasped. My eyes fixated on his lips. It felt hot. So hot.

Eric's gaze burned into me. Desire ignited within their depths as he pressed his lips to mine. Only softly. Only once. A rush of air escaped my lungs when he pulled away. Eric's lips curled into a smile. My mind floated on the feelings stirring within me. His lips pressed to my ear as he did things that made me want him even more.

Whispering in my ear, he said, "We're the same. Whether you admit it or not, we are the same."

His words swam in my head. I didn't answer. I only pulled him closer. His lips slid over my neck, making my knees buckle. To keep me from falling, Eric thrust me into the wall pinning his body onto mine. My back slammed against the plaster, as Eric's body pressed into me. The jolt made me feel like this was wrong. I shouldn't be here like this, but I couldn't remember why.

Eric's hands slid over my body, as he pressed his mouth to mine. This time he kissed me, opening his mouth as I wanted. My lips parted and his tongue swept against mine, gently. He teased and tasted my mouth in small kisses that were driving me insane. My stomach flipped as his hands moved over my waist, and slid down my back. But, it wasn't enough. I needed him. I needed more. My arms laced behind his neck, and Eric glided his hands over my body feeling every curve beneath his palms. My body responded to his touch, gently pushing into his hands as they caressed me. Eric suddenly broke the kiss, and grabbed my wrists from his neck. He held them over my head and pressed me into the wall. Heart pounding, I gasped. My body writhed beneath him, longing for his touch. Longing for him.

Eric's breathing was jagged. He pressed his forehead down to mine, while keeping my arms pinned above my head. He laughed, "And I thought that you could resist me?" His eyes slipped down to my chest, and I pressed against him. "Do you want me, Ivy?" My eyes were wide, fixated on his face. I didn't understand why he was speaking. I wanted his lips on mine. He knew I wanted him. As if he could read my mind, Eric lowered his face, and his soft lips brushed my neck. I moaned. A smile twisted his lips. "We're the same, because we see what we want—and we take it. And right now… I want you."

CHAPTER FOUR

Eric's lips pressed down on my mouth, but a scream erupted from my throat. He pulled back, and looked at me. His words stoked the dying embers of my brain, cracking the lust with lies. With a forceful shove, I untangled us, and pushed him away.

Pointing my blade toward him, I screamed, "We are NOT the same!" My entire body was red, covered in a blush that I couldn't conceal. And I hated him for it. I hated what he did to me. And why he thought we were alike was incomprehensible.

His gaze was intense, still burning for me. "We are. You just haven't accepted it, yet." He took another step toward me, ignoring my weapon. "You just… " He didn't get to finish his sentence. I lunged my left arm forward as if I fought with this hand all the time. The movement made him stop. The smile slid off his face.

"We are not the same!" I screamed. "You killed her! It was you! I trusted you! I said there was something different about you!" The night of Al's death rushed back into my mind. A string of a hundred images played back to back, and I couldn't make them stop. My fingers pressed against my temples for a split second as I tried to stop the memory onslaught.

Eric stepped toward me. "There is," he answered.

But I didn't let him say more. My hands fell back into an attacker's position, and I jabbed the blades toward his chest. "There is not." I snarled. "I was wrong. I was wrong about me and I was wrong about you." I held my ground. I needed more time. The rage burned off the lust for now, but my right hand was too weak to grip the blade. I'd need to throw some force into the lunge if I was to pierce his heart. It was the only way to kill him.

Time. I needed more time, but his words confused me. They awoke the lust he made me feel. Eric's touch made me a mindless slave. I spoke, not caring what I said as long as it held him back and kept him silent. "I don't need your help. I can figure out what's on that page from your book without you. To think you even remembered was... " I shook my head, not bothering to finish my sentence. "You're right, Eric. I am a fool. There is no trusting demons. There is no compassion, no kindness, no love left in your putrid body. I'm the one who did this to you and I'm the one who will end it."

While I was speaking I could feel the rage seeping from the depths of my soul and filling every part of my body. My eyes pooled violet and I ignored it, thinking I could control myself, but the longer I spoke the more I began to question why I shouldn't let the rage overtake me. Al had warned me not to. She told Eric to teach me how to contain it, but I didn't want to. Not now. Rage held power—power I needed to kill Eric. After my eyes pooled, I felt tingling in my right hand. The skin was smooth, and crusted in blood. My blood. Drawing my hands together, I switched my weapon into my right hand. Eric watched me do it. Every muscle in my body felt like it was on fire. White hot fury washed through me with a deafening roar. I didn't hear Eric's words. His lust had no power over me in that moment. He no longer tried to move towards me. His words held no seduction.

I lunged at him, swiping my weapon at his throat.

Eric spoke, but I failed to hear him. I swung and he dodged. A strange familiarity came over me as I fought him. We'd done this before, long ago. His golden eyes would dance as he fought me back then, and I would lose. I lost every time. Eric had been a warrior. He taught me to fight. He taught me to win. We'd run through the old gym at the church like children on a playground. Without a doubt, I knew Eric wouldn't hurt me back then. Nothing was real at that time. Demons and angels were some distant thing that I would never encounter. I didn't realize how deep I'd gotten. Eric was kind then. He helped me. He knew me. And I had no idea what I'd do to him. I had no idea how much pain I would inflict on him before his life ended. It made my heart sink long enough to hear what he was saying.

My mind jumped out of the past. The memories blew away like a feather in the wind. When the memory faded I realized that my body had been swinging my weapon, and attacking without thought. It seemed that my anger put me on autopilot. My advances were innate. I swung. I blocked. I attacked. Nothing was planned. And as Eric's voice drifted up to my ears, I found that I'd beaten him. I'd inflicted wounds that I didn't remember giving. Blood streaked his face dripping down his cheeks and into his hair as he lay beneath me. My legs straddled him, pinning Eric to the ground. He didn't wince, or close his eyes. Instead he kept speaking words I couldn't hear. Words that sputtered beneath a sea of static. I watched his lips move, as I swung my arms over my head. My back arched with my blade secure in both hands. Poised to strike. Ready to kill. All I had to do was plunge my blades down and into his heart.

Eric's words cut through the haze of rage for a split second, and I heard him. "… cannot defeat him on your own. He'll use you Ivy. He'll make you into something you're not. Fuck! Wake up! Listen to me!"

I paused, staring down at him, feeling my arms tremble as I held them still over my head. I wondered how I pinned him. I didn't remember this. I didn't recall throwing Eric to the floor. I was ready to strike and end his words forever, but something stopped me. It was like someone *paused* me.

His eyes were completely golden, without a bit of red. His voice was soft, neither pleading nor panicked. "I remember you. I remember who you are even if you don't… Ivy, let go of the rage. Let it go and come back to me."

In that second, my resolve hardened. There was no mercy, no forgiveness for what he'd done. And the fact that I'd made him what he was, was even worse. It was time to end this. It was time to end the pain I'd caused by trying to make him into something he wasn't. By trying to save him. Every muscle in my body burned and I felt myself becoming more drained by the second. A scream erupted from deep within me and ripped out of my throat. Eric pressed his eyes closed, as my weapon swung straight towards his heart. As the silvery tip touched his flesh, I expected it to rip through him like a tissue.

But it did not. When my blade hit Eric's chest the tip touched his flesh, sinking in slightly and then stopped. Eric's eyes went wide, but he said nothing. Enraged, I threw my arms over my head for the second time. Not understanding what happened, I swung down a second time. There was no saving him from this. Eric would die. As the tines whistled through the air downward toward Eric's chest, I felt something grab me. It felt like I was snatched from the spot where I pinned Eric to the ground. Mid-swing, I was pelted with cold air. Colors of light streaked past me so fast that all I could do was scream. It felt like I'd fallen into a black hole. The world rushed past me in a streak of colors and meaningless sounds. They continued to blare by without pause. Until it stopped. Then, with an ungodly thud, I landed on a slick golden floor. My comb clattered next to me with the blades retracted. A black boot stepped towards me, as a hand reached down and pulled me up by my shirt.

"Have you lost your mind?" Lorren screamed at me. My fingers wrapped around his grip trying to pull him off of me, but he tossed me across the room like I was nothing. I hit the golden floor of the Lorren.

CHAPTER FIVE

Rage poured out of my mouth, as I shot off the ground and ran at him. "I was about to kill him! You had no right to… "

As I collided with Lorren, he grabbed my wrists, jerked more towards him and spat angrily in my face. "I had every right. You can't screw this up. I'll kill you myself, if you do. Look at yourself. Do you even know what you've done? You allowed your rage to consume you. Look!"

He thrust me towards a golden mirror. My reflection was… horrifying. Shaking my head, I couldn't breathe. All the air was sucked out of my lungs as I stared at myself. Dried blood covered my torn clothes and dirt-streaked face. Long blue patches wrapped around my throat in three long bands— bruises from Eric's grip on my neck. The blood and the bruises weren't what made me gasp. That wasn't the most disturbing thing. When I stopped struggling, Lorren released me. I moved slowly towards the glass as if it were made of poison.

My jaw hung open as my hands touched my face. Pure violet eyes gazed back. Long curling tongues of flame, that used to be my dark hair, lifted around my face. The flames glowed and danced like Medusa's snakes swaying in a breeze that didn't exist. Black marks marred my pale skin in small patches that resembled tiny gleaming scales. When I touched the black flesh, it felt cold and slick beneath my fingers.

Trembling my hand fell to my side. I turned back to Lorren with wide, pleading eyes. "What did this? What's happening to me?" I stared at him for a moment hoping he'd show me compassion that I didn't deserve.

He rolled his dark eyes, and grabbed my shoulders. Twisting me back towards the mirror, he pushed me forward and said, "Look once, and look hard. I will never offer you this again. Rage is poison, Ivy. It flows through your body and corrupts everything you are. You're becoming what you feared the most—demonic. You hair will turn to snakes, your skin will turn to scales, and your eyes will burn with hate." He twisted me back towards him. Tears streaked down my cheeks, and I couldn't bear to look at him. He shook me once. Hard. "Never forget who you are. Vengeance is not justice. I put Eric and Al on your path to help you. You completely screwed up Eric, but Al knew it was her time."

"What?" I squeaked, feeling the last rush of anger leave me.

Lorren didn't look at me. Instead he moved around in the golden chamber, sifting through some loose things on a table. I had no idea what they were—they were odd shapes—and looked to be made of glass. Lorren picked one up and walked over to me. "They were both chosen a long time ago to make certain that Kreturus does not win. Al did her job. Kreturus played you. And you let him." Lorren cracked one of the glass beads and poured its cold contents over my head. It sank into the flames that had been my hair, and cooled them. Soon the flickering violet flames became still, lying limp on top of my head.

"He played me? How? I haven't even seen him. Not since I was down here." I looked at Lorren and I could tell that he had no more patience with me. This was the end of it.

He spun me around again, and forced me to sit on a golden stool. He cracked another glass gem over my head. I didn't dare move, even when it felt like bugs creeping down into my scalp. "He's been following you, influencing those around you. He still wants you, Ivy. That will never change. When Al saw Eric in the clearing, she knew that the demon was influencing him. Eric didn't act of his own accord. Kreturus' hand forced him. Yes, Eric wanted the book. Yes, he has it. And yes, Al saw the manipulation. That is why she didn't want you to go. You weren't ready to face Kreturus. She gave her life to spare yours. She knew you still need Eric."

Dazed, I stared straight ahead and said nothing. My scalp tingled as the unseen substance spread over my head. I replayed that night in my mind. Lorren remained silent allowing me to peruse my thoughts. Eric had been acting oddly. Even for the Valefar version of him. I didn't understand why. I'd assumed that I'd misjudged him. I thought I was wrong about him. And the cost was Al's life. But according to Lorren, there was more going on than I could see. I glanced at my hands, turning them over, avoiding Lorren's eye, "So, all that time, Kreturus was nearby?"

He knelt next to me, and when I looked up at him there was hope shining in Lorren's eyes. "Yes. He'll never leave you alone. He's there, silently stalking you—waiting to pounce. This outburst almost gave him the opportunity. If you'd killed Eric and allowed the rage to permanently consume you—you'd be with him now." Horrified, I stared at Lorren with my jaw hanging open. "They both told you to control your anger. They both warned you several times… "

"How did you know?" I didn't doubt his words, but wanted to know if he was there the way Kreturus had been. I knew nothing about angels, and Lorren was one. "Were you there all along and I didn't see you?"

At first Lorren didn't reply. His dark hair hung in his eyes as he reached for another glass stone and cracked it, pouring its contents onto my head. Then he pushed his finger into the cavity of the glass, and smeared some of the colored goo on the skin that was now black scales. He touched it to my shoulder, the base of my neck, and slid the last bit across my left cheek. He looked into my face for a moment, then turned and sat down.

After throwing the empty piece of glass on the table he said, "I can see you. I'm an angel, and could have followed you, but I can't leave here." I went to open my mouth to ask why not, but he cut me off. "Don't ask. I won't tell you. It doesn't affect your fate, only mine. I used the glass to see where you were and what you were doing." He shook his head. "When you get off course, there is no middle road for you, huh? It's crash and burn all the way."

I stared at him for a moment. He was so odd. I wanted to know why he was trapped in the Lorren, but couldn't ask. I leaned forward to stretch my back, and buried my face in my hands. When I sat up, I pushed brown hair away out of my eyes. Surprised, I grasped a brown curl between my fingers and looked at it. There was no trace of the flames. I glanced at Lorren, who was watching me intently. "You fixed it?"

He nodded. "It's easier to remember who you are when you can still see it. But there are no second chances. Not anymore. That was nearly permanent, and I do not have the power to intervene like that again." Lorren was silent for a moment, and moved closer, locking his dark eyes with mine. "You can *not* kill Eric. Period. He has my protection, no matter what form he's in."

My jaw dropped. "How? How could you protect him? He killed Al. She was a good person. He isn't!" I felt anger course through me. I resisted the urge to grab it and hold onto it. Lorren watched me as I let the feeling subside.

"Mmmm," his voice was deep. "What if things weren't as you understood them? What if Al gave her life and Eric was the unlucky guy who got stuck holding the sword?" He rose and walked towards me. His face said he spoke the truth, although I couldn't possibly understand how that could be. He stopped in front of me. "See with your heart. It's the ability that will save you. It's the gift Al knew you had. She said that your passions would damn you, but that she knew your heart could overcome anything thrown at you. She said you were strong. She knew you could do this." Lorren's dark gaze rested on my face. I wanted to squirm.

"You speak of her like she's still alive… " I glanced up at him. "Don't you mourn the dead?"

"Don't assume to know me, Ivy Taylor." Lorren bit the words at me, and turned away. He walked back to the table and sat on the top, swinging his legs off the side. He still wore solid black clothing that seemed too big for him. His dark hair hung in his eyes. It was quiet for several minutes before he spoke again. "What of your wound? Why didn't you do as I told you?"

Pressing my lips together, I looked away from him. I found I was speaking before I knew what I would say, "I can't. I can't do that to him. Surely you can understand. You spared Eric."

But he shook his head, "No, I don't understand. Collin didn't serve angels for centuries upon centuries. He didn't risk his life to save others. He allowed Kreturus to use him and manipulate you. And yet, you could kill Eric, but not Collin?" He arched a dark eyebrow at me.

My face scrunched tightly as I was about to spew out words. When I realized there would be no convincing him, I turned my head away and said nothing.

Lorren finally spoke, "The ending is the same for him, Ivy, whether you do it now or later. Collin's a Valefar. Stay away from him."

I stood, and looked at Lorren. "Al trusted him. Why can't you?"

"Al was human and prone to making mistakes. That is a luxury that you no longer have. Stay away from him Ivy." When I didn't answer, he added, "I've made it so that you cannot kiss him again—not without taking your soul back."

"What?" I shouted at him, rounding on him. Every muscle in my body tensed.

He rose and walked towards me. Lorren towered over me, and crouched slightly so we were eye to eye. The gesture made me want to punch him. "I'm forcing you to do what you must to survive. One of the gems I healed you with will seek out to repair you fully. You cannot stop it. You have to defeat Kreturus. And you can't do it half healed. Every second your soul is in that boy is another second that gives Kreturus the opportunity to defeat all of us—without a fight." He stood and looked down at me, sliding his hands into his pockets. "I removed the traces of demon scales and burning snakes. Do not allow them to return. I don't want to see you again until you have your soul back."

CHAPTER SIX

Lorren was difficult, but I had very few allies left. Apparently psychotic Eric was an ally, which was hard to swallow. If an angel hadn't told me, I wouldn't have believed it. As it was, I didn't want to believe it. It was much easier to hate Eric for killing Al than it was to try and understand what was happening around me. Angels and demons didn't think like people. They did things, things that I didn't understand. And instead of trying to fathom it, I forced myself to accept Lorren's words as truth. Although that didn't mean I'd forgiven Eric.

Once again, I found myself moving through the Underworld alone. Lorren sucked me down here with his fancy angel magic, but he couldn't put me back. I had to walk out. Maybe he knew it would allow my anger to burn off by the time I reached the portal. As I walked, I wondered why Lorren was trapped down here. It was something I couldn't accept if it happened to me. To never have the sunlight on my face again— the thought was unbearable. This place was filled with shadows so thick they seemed to breathe. A lacy shadow covered my body in a blink and was gone. When I looked around, nothing was there. A tingle ran up my back, and I kept looking over my shoulder. It felt like someone was watching me. I quickened my pace. My feet bled leaving a trail of stained stones behind me. The screech of grackles lingered in the distance. When I turned back to see how far away the demon birds were, I slipped and came crashing down. The knee of my jeans tore open. Cursing, I rose and looked for the birds. But there was no sight of them. I walked faster.

Staring at the Underworld made it easy to think. This is where I was supposed to rule. This ungodly portion of land was what Kreturus ruled for eons. Shaking my head, I realized that it was time. It was time to stop playing—time to step up and accept who and what I was. I am the Prophecy One—the Demon Queen. The thought made me uneasy. It was like admitting that I failed, but part of me longed for the peace it would bring. Accepting the prophecy meant that I'd accepted myself. I once knew who I was. I was a sister, and a daughter. I was kind and smart. But now, I had no idea. Accepting my role and accepting the fact that I'd defeat an ancient demon scared the hell out of me. But I no longer thought of it as someone else's life. This was my life. I was surrounded by Valefar, Martis, demons, and angels. And I was getting used to it.

Sitting down on a large stone, I grabbed my bare foot and rubbed it. Although my skin healed fast, walking through the rocky ground barefoot was ripping my feet apart. Sitting for a second would allow them to heal enough to keep moving. I glanced around me. Rust colored stone surrounded me. The sound of water dripping was louder than the screech of birds. I swallowed. Without realizing it, I was sitting on the stone where I saw Collin when he thought I was dead. I remembered the slump of his shoulders and the void in his eyes. Pressing my eyes closed, I shook my head and stood. I couldn't ever see him again. I didn't know how I'd keep him away, but I had to. I had to buy enough time to find Satan's Stone. If I could find it, I could use it to heal me, and then I wouldn't need my soul back. Collin would survive with his scrap of soul and mine. I hadn't forgiven him for using his blood on me, and didn't know if I could, but I couldn't give him a demon kiss. It didn't matter what Lorren did to me. I couldn't.

A lacy shadow spread over my body, slowly sliding across me like a blanket. I looked up. My heart constricted and rose into my throat, until I realized it was the dragon-stalker that'd been following me last time I was down here. She landed next to me like a giant cat.

"Why are you following me?" I gazed at her, but her ruby eyes held no answer. She gazed at me, as if she wanted something, but I didn't know what.

I looked at my bare feet and then back at her ruby-colored eyes. Riding would be far less painful. And she kept the demons and grackles away. I still didn't understand why she followed me, but it didn't matter right then.

I stood and walked over to her, running my hand along her scaly face. "Why are you here? You seem to show up at strange times, and I have no idea if I'm supposed to talk to you or what…" It felt like she should be the equivalent of a cat—a really smart one—but still an animal. But something about her made me feel like she wasn't an animal at all.

The dragon lowered her head, and slowly pushed at me with her maw until I climbed on her back. When I was in place, I dug my fingers around a scale to keep from falling off. It didn't seem to hurt her. Taking a step forward, she lurched rather gracelessly and took off, much like a flying cow. "Where are you taking me?" I asked as she turned the wrong way. But she kept flying, ignoring my tugs to turn around.

We flew past the jagged rocks below and over the unforgiving terrain. The wind rushed by, pulling at my hair like giant fingers. She slowed and landed in a part of the Underworld I'd yet to see. Darkness clung to every corner, and the rust colored rocks seemed to hum with a life of their own. Small sounds shifted through the shadows, but when I looked nothing was there.

She took me to a different set of catacombs—a different portal out of the Underworld. When I slid off her back, I moved slowly toward the portal wondering why she took me to this exit. I asked her over my shoulder, "Why'd you take me here?" But when I turned around, she was already gone.

The sound of sand skittering across rock made me pause. Twisting on my foot, I touched my comb to my mark and extended the deadly blades. The silver tines grew in my hand as I peered through the darkness at my attacker. Dull green eyes started at me. The sound of my racing heart pounded in my ears. I stared at her wondering if she still recognized me. Her black blade was drawn and her body was half crouching as if she was ready to attack, but she hesitated. The look of confusion that lined her face held me in place.

Apryl.

Her eyes narrowed as she studied my face. Finally she asked, "Ivy?" At the moment she asked my name, the rigidness in her spine melted, and her weapon slid to her side. Her brow pinched together as she looked behind me and then back at my face. "What are you doing here?"

"I had to get... ," I paused realizing that I shouldn't tell her about Lorren. An angel in Hell—well he was already in a precarious situation. I didn't want to do anything to make it worse. "I needed something from the Lorren." She didn't detect the lie. "Then the dragon dumped me here. I didn't have much of a choice." After a moment, I asked, "What are you doing here? I thought you were bound to the Pool of Lost Souls? It's not nearby, is it?" I turned my head, glancing around, still trying to figure out where we were.

Her hair seemed more brown than red in the darkness. She wore the same outfit I saw her in last time, a nondescript pair of jeans and a tee shirt that had once been white. She would have traded them in for a dress, before she was turned Valefar. Now, I wondered if she would don a skirt over pants. I wondered how much of my sister remained behind those eyes. Either way, it was good to see her, even if she didn't remember our past. It saved her from experiencing the pain of our mother's death, the loss of our childhood home... and the realization that her sister was the antichrist.

Apryl's wide green eyes gazed at the stone walls like she didn't know where she was. After watching her mannerisms for a moment it seemed like she was dazed. The longer I watched her, the more certain I became. Apryl was acting like a person who was hit by a car and kept on walking, unable to deal with the trauma.

She bit her lower lip, "We're not by the Pool of Lost Souls." She blinked hard, as if trying to remember something that was just out of reach. When she looked at me she said, "I was. I am bound to the Pool. But, something happened, and now I'm here. He carried me here..." The fingers of her right hand pressed to her temples.

I lowered my comb, but didn't retract the silver blades. Something was wrong. I'd never seen a disoriented Valefar. It didn't seem to bother them in the slightest if they didn't know where they were, as long as there were souls nearby to feed from. Cautiously, I stepped toward her, asking, "What happened? What happened at the Pool?"

She lowered her hand and glanced around. It was as if she were afraid something had followed her. I peered through the shadows surrounding us, but saw nothing. However I had the haunting suspicion that we were being watched. It made a chill rake my spine and I shivered. Her green eyes looked back at me, "I don't know. One moment we were both there, and the next, we weren't."

She wasn't making any sense. "Who?" Apryl didn't answer. She seemed to not realize I was standing in front of her. I took a step closer, and when she didn't respond, I put my hands on her shoulders. Unblinking green eyes peered into mine. I asked again, "Who's we, Apryl?"

She pressed her lips together. "Me and the Guardian."

My hands dropped from her shoulders, as my eyes widened. Alarm shot through me as I took a step away from her. "But… " I shook my head trying to get through the torrent of thoughts sloshing through my mind. "But, that can't be. The Guardian couldn't leave. He was the one guarding the portal. He's the one who keeps the Underworld, under the world, and separate." I squeaked the last part, but Apryl's daze didn't fade. She gazed around the room, seemingly seeing things of interest that didn't exist. I placed my hands on her shoulders again to get her attention. Her dull eyes met mine. "Is he dead?" The thought frightened me more than anything else. I was unable to kill the thing, so whoever did this was more powerful than me by far. When she didn't answer, I pressed my fingers tighter into her shoulder, "Apryl. Is he dead?"

Apryl twisted her shoulders and I released my grasp on her. Her hands moved frantically, as she shook her head. "I don't know. I can't remember a thing. I can't… Remember." She looked up at me with vacant eyes, eyes that had seen too much.

I glanced over her shoulder. The feeling that we were being watched didn't subside. There was still someone there, listening. Waiting. I wrapped my arm around her shoulders, and began to usher her towards the portal. "You're coming with me."

Apryl followed me until I spoke, at which point her feet came to an abrupt stop. She shook her head from side to side. "I can't leave. I can't! Ivy, don't make me." She bent over screaming, pressing her fingers to the sides of her head. Something behind her moved. I didn't need any more reasons to run. I wrapped my fingers around her arm and pulled her to the portal. I placed my pendant in the tiny slot and the tomb slid opened. Shoving a shivering Apryl ahead of me, we stepped over the threshold and the stone tomb slid shut behind us.

CHAPTER SEVEN

Gazing into the darkness, I couldn't tell what I was looking at. Above us was a massive slab of white marble veined with pewter. And nothing else. The door to the Underworld was at my back. Apryl was squashed next to me. We were trapped inside a tomb, encased in marble. My heart began to race as the tight space seemed to shrink. Apryl was half hysterical already and muttering to herself words that I couldn't understand. I told her it would be alright and began to try and slide my fingers around the edges of the marble, but there was no way I could lift it. Normally, I would have effonated away from this point, but I couldn't. Cold fear began to pool in my stomach as I stared at the stone. I couldn't get out of the tomb.

Apryl's mutterings soon stopped when she seemed to realize that we were stuck. She sniffled and said, "*Portos Uglamaya.*" When she touched the stone with her hand, her arm passed through the solid rock. It was if the marble had turned to milk. She retracted her hand and looked at me. "You're a shitty Valefar." A smirk crossed her lips as she shook off the rest of the somber haze. The marble rippled as my breath crossed the surface of the stone. "You're right. It's time to get out of here." And without another word, she shoved me into the stone.

Panic shot through me as the cold stone surrounded me. I couldn't breathe. I couldn't scream. Silken liquid stone flowed around me as I moved through the space. The rapid beat of my heart echoed in my ears, as I frantically moved forward, half walking, half swimming, trying to get out. The cool stone slid over my skin without pause, always moving, always flowing. Just when I didn't think I could stand it for another moment, a hand grabbed my shoulder and jerked me out of the milky stone. I fell on the dark slate floor inside the mausoleum. The marble tomb we were trapped in moments ago was at my side. Apryl stood next to me and I was on my butt at her feet.

"You can't stay in there. What's the matter with you?" she asked. She looked down at me like I was an idiot.

Sliding my legs under me, I rose and brushed off my jeans. "I've never done that before. What did you do?"

She arched an eyebrow at me in disbelief. The corner of her mouth twitched into a smile. "You are a Valefar, aren't you? I mean, you smell weird, but you don't smell human either. And you aren't Martis?" I shook my head and sneered as she said Martis. "Then what are you? Because if you were a Valefar, you could do basic things. Even with my brain half drugged, I could do it."

"You were drugged? That's why you were so despondent?" My brows bunched together as I stared at her. She seemed normal again, well normal for the Valefar version of Apryl.

She nodded, "Yeah, something like that. I can't remember what cut me loose from the Pool, but I remember that the Guardian and I were both there, and then we weren't. After that I wandered around unaware of dangers around me or where I was going. It felt like something was following me—herding me towards that portal. My mental abilities were," she paused, searching for the correct word, "addled. I couldn't think. It felt like my mind was wrapped in a sheet of plastic and suffocating. When you pulled me through the portal, it lifted and I slowly realized what was happening. Which brings us back to you… " She cocked her hip and tilted her head at me. "Why couldn't you drag us through the stone?"

I folded my arms over my chest and gazed around the large tomb. There was another stone door that we had to pass through to get outside. My eyes cut back toward Apryl. "I'm not a Valefar. I'm half. Half Valefar. Half Martis. The Valefar are trying to trap me. The Martis are trying to kill me. I have a Seeker after me, who used to be my best friend. And I accidentally turned a good Martis into a psychotic Valefar. He also wants to kill me, but it seems he'd rather torture me first." Apryl's jaw slowly dropped as I spoke. Her brows sliding further up her face as the list of crazy people following me got longer and longer. "I'm not good company. Not unless you have a death wish, but I couldn't leave you there either. Not like that."

She nodded towards the exterior marble door. It towered above us and hung on hinges the size of my head. "Take us through the door."

I grumbled at her, "I can't. I'm only half Valefar. I can't do that stuff."

She snorted, "Yes, you can. Who told you that you couldn't?" She sighed. "You're such a dope sometimes, Ivy. Think about it. You have demon blood flowing through you—why couldn't you command it the same way the Valefar do? You'd have to pay the same price, but other than that—why couldn't you?"

Looking at the massive door, I unfolded my arms and walked towards it. I'd never thought about it really. Collin had forbidden me from using anything other than the two things he taught me. He'd said the price was too high. Turning back to Apryl I asked, "What's the price for turning the door to milk?"

She laughed, "There is no set price. It's more of a sliding scale, based on ability and age. You're too new for it to cost more than you have." She studied me for a moment, and then walked toward the door. "Dark magic is always paid for in pain. Pain and power." Her fingers pressed against the cold stone. She spoke as she traced the pattern carved into the marble. "It's the way of things. Every ability has a pain price. It's usually close to the person's pain threshold. He made it that way—so that the person wielding the magic feels every ounce of pain and doesn't have the luxury of passing out." She turned to me. Her hair fell over her shoulder. "The power price is different. I have no power, so it cost me nothing. I'm the lowest of the slaves. You can't get lower." She started to speak and then stopped. She pressed her fingers once more to the stone, and then withdrew her hand. When she turned back to me she said, "How can he take a power price from you, if he has no control over you?"

"What do you mean?" I asked.

Apryl walked around the room. The white marble appeared gray in the darkness. She stood in front of the ornate stone, slowly walking the perimeter of the room thinking. She didn't seem like the old Apryl and I wasn't foolish enough to think I could trust her, but she was telling me things that no one else had. And I could speak to her without the mental haze of blood lust. Damn, Eric. I still wanted to hurt him, even if I couldn't kill him.

I turned my attention back to Apryl as she asked, "Well, he doesn't. Does he?" She walked towards me, crossing the space in three strides. "Kreturus has been waiting for you to go to him, right? He didn't force you?"

"He said he didn't want to." I paused, realizing how stupid that sounded. "He can't force me, can he? The only way for him to use my power is if I surrender. He can't use it otherwise. So I'd only pay the pain price to use Valefar magic, not the power price, right?" I gazed at Apryl.

She shrugged. "There's only one way to find out. Go through the door." She pointed at the mass of marble. "I'll meet you on the other side."

"Wait!" She turned and looked at me. I asked, "Why don't you effonate? Why do this instead?"

She smirked at me. "Effonation has a high price in power and pain. If Kreturus took the power price from you, you'd know it as clearly as you know the pain of using the magic." Shaking her head she moved toward me, and folded her arms across her chest. "You can effonate? And you have?" I nodded. Her lips parted as if she was going to speak, but she snapped her mouth shut and shook her head. "So effonate through the door."

"I can't. Well, I can, but… " my voice trailed off.

"But what?" Apryl's gaze cut into me. "We're wasting time. In case you didn't notice, something was watching us back there. We shouldn't stay here. It's right on the other side of the portal, and since I don't have any memory of what happened to me—I don't know what it is. Come on. Time to go." She tugged at me.

"I can't. I have to… " She stopped pulling me and turned to look at me. "I'm wounded. I have sapphire serum in my chest." I pointed to the remaining poison near to my heart. "I can't effonate. I keep getting spliced and it hurts like hell. Plus, I don't have any way to heal it."

Apryl's eyes were wide. "Shit, girl." Without another word, she wrapped her fingers around my wrist and shoved me forward. I almost protested when she slammed me into the stone, but it turned soft right as my face hit it. I sank through like before and tried to swim across to the other side. Since I knew what was happening this time, I allowed my instincts to take over. My feet stopped kicking and settled on the bottom of the liquid stone. I took two steps forward, much like walking through a vat of paste, and stepped out into the night air. A cold gust of rainy wind hit my face as I gasped for air.

Apryl stood in front of me dripping. "You figured it out. Good. Now, let's get out of here so we can figure out what's going on."

CHAPTER EIGHT

The graveyard was muddy from several days of rain and we were soaked. As we walked through the old tombstones and trees, I could hear cars echoing somewhere nearby. I stooped to read one of the granite stones. Most of the letters were worn away by the elements. It took two to three stones to be certain we were where I thought.

"I know where we are," I told her. We were in an old cemetery from the 1600's that sat high on a hill a mile or so from where we grew up. Apryl wouldn't remember, but I did. We used to come out here in the summer to read the epitaphs between sprigs of flowers. The dragon must have brought me to this portal on purpose, but I wasn't sure why. Besides that he seems to have led Apryl there, too. I followed the sound to the road, with Apryl walking behind me. Then we walked to an abandoned warehouse a few blocks away.

Apryl followed me without question. I didn't like this. I didn't like her being a Valefar. It was a risk to keep her around because Kreturus could use her any time he wanted. At least I thought he could. I still wasn't certain how he was moving around. I decided to keep her with me because Apryl was right before. Kreturus had no control over me. He couldn't touch my power by using demon magic. I was certain of it, because if effonating had a high power price, I would have noticed. I sure as hell noticed the pain. No, Kreturus didn't have control over me. But then that meant he had control over every other Valefar. He could be anywhere. He could use any of them, except Collin. Collin's mark was purple, like mine. That made him belong to no one, but I couldn't be completely certain. I could only hope.

The warehouse was dank and dark. The metal roof sounded like marbles were falling on it instead of rain. We settled down on the floor. There were some crates in the corners with reams of paper that went to waste. I was so tired that I could barely sit up. Apryl said, "You look weak." I didn't reply. I couldn't sleep. Not here. Not now. I was unguarded from both Martis and

Valefar—plus I had one sitting next to me. "Is it the poison?"

I yawned, and nodded. "It should have killed me, you know. I shouldn't be here. That was the second time I should have died this year, and instead—I'm here with you." Maybe it was foolish to tell her, but I didn't think stating the obvious put me in any more danger than I was already in. She had eyes after all, and could see I was about to pass out from exhaustion.

She nodded. "Then sleep." I shot her a look from under my brow. She laughed. "What could I possibly do? You're far stronger than I am, even weakened like this. I can't effonate on my best day. But, I do need to… " she paused and grimaced. "I need to eat. Rest, Ivy. I'll be back in a while, and then we can talk. I have a feeling that your Valefar 101 classes were skipped."

CHAPTER NINE

I was so sore and tired that I fell asleep almost instantly. The entire time I slept, my dreams were filled with blood and screaming souls. Death ravaged my mind and pulled on my emotions until I cried out in my sleep. With a jerk, I shot upright trying to get my bearings as my scream faded into soft echoes at the back of the warehouse. The silver comb was clutched tightly in my grip. My heart was racing in my chest, as the back of my neck prickled.

Someone was there, and it wasn't Apryl. I could hear his breath, the slow intake of air as he tried to maintain his composure. The sound was near silent. It came from the very back of the warehouse where the shadows were thick like tar. His body was hidden from sight, but the bond tugged tightly, pulling at my gut. I knew who it was. My muscles relaxed slightly as I rose.

Peering through the darkness, I looked but couldn't see him. Finally I called out, "Go away. I know you're here and I don't want to see you."

Collin emerged from the darkness, dropping whatever shroud concealed him and moved toward me. My throat tightened. Additional worry creased my brow with each step of his foot. Fear surged through me in an icy cold blast. I was afraid of what Lorren did to me. It didn't know if it was something that would make me savagely rip my soul from his body, and I didn't want to find out. I had enough lust induced insanity for one day.

Panicked, I started to step away from him and screamed, "STOP!"

Collin's feet abruptly immobilized. His head tilted to the side slightly, not certain what to think of the fear that was wafting off of me. I knew he could sense it. I knew the bond told him that I was afraid. He looked at me from across the room with a sea of cement separating us. Industrial lighting hung above, suspended from rusty rafters, but failed to illuminate the room. We stared at each other in the darkness, each of us waiting for the other to move or speak.

As my heart thumped in my chest, I wrung my hands waiting for something to happen—something to change. But it didn't. Nothing felt different. But I didn't trust myself, not without knowing exactly what Lorren had done to me. He told me I wouldn't be able to kiss Collin again without taking my soul back. I didn't know what that entailed.

And I didn't trust Collin.

My arms folded tightly across my chest, and I tucked my hands into the crooks of my elbows to prevent him from seeing them shake. His presence sent my heart racing—being this close to him made me want to feel his strong hands sliding across my skin. If Lorren made that worse, in any way, I'd be unable to help myself.

Collin's hands fell to his sides as his mouth opened, "Ivy… " His voice was rich and deep. It was the perfect blend of confidence and compassion. The sound made me want to go to him. It made me want to forget the betrayal. It made me want to forget Lorren, and everything else. I'd give anything to have him hold me in his strong arms—the way things used to be. I yearned for it so deeply, but I suppressed the desires before they'd fully formed in my mind. The bond would allow these feelings to slip through more easily if they were full thoughts. But as non-contemplated desires—he would have to intentionally enter my mind to feel them.

I wrapped my arms around my middle. With a deep breath, I turned my back on him, and hung my head low as I gazed at the filthy floor. "Go away." My hair fell over my shoulder as I whispered the words. I expected him to leave. I expected him to speak. But I failed to expect what he actually did. Before I had a chance to blink he was behind me. I felt the rush of wind at my back from his sudden movement, and I turned on the ball of my foot. My hair swirled around, flying over my shoulders when I suddenly stopped. The silver comb was in my hand ready to strike.

Collin stopped an inch from my face. I sucked in air, surprised. His warm breath washed across my skin as he tried to control himself. "No," he answered, his deep voice resonating with determination. Sapphire eyes bore into me with such intensity that I wanted to look away. They were that deep blue, the blue his eyes turned when Collin was teetering on the edge of the crazy line. A muscle in my jaw flinched. His eyes darted to the spot as his gaze slipped over my body, taking in the tension throughout. The curve of his lips was nearly absent as his mouth moved into a straight line. "I have to tell you. I have to explain."

He was too close. Our faces were less than an inch apart and our bodies were even closer. One deep breath and my chest would brush against his. My stomach twisted inside of me. Lorren's words rang in my ears.

I've made it so you'll have to take your soul back. I'd have no choice if Collin kissed me. Desire would flood through me with a seduction too powerful to deny. My breath caught in my throat, as I broke eye contact and slid my foot away. But Collin moved forward filling the void with his body.

"Then explain," I said refusing to look him in the eye. He spoke, and I tried to listen. His words were urgent and pleading, but I couldn't listen. I couldn't look at him.

Terror coursed through me in unrelenting waves, each more powerful than the first. Collin's voice continued to flow at a rushed pace, as he could see and feel my reaction. He knew that I wanted him to leave, he just didn't know why. While he spoke the intensity of his emotions cut through the panic that was choking me. Desperation laced his thoughts, but he was confident that I'd forgive him. He saw this conversation ending with a vivid picture in his mind.

A picture that I couldn't allow.

When he stopped speaking, I noticed it—the faint scent, sweet and seductive, coming from him. It was on his skin, in his hair, and on his breath. Inhaling slightly, I tried to identify what it was. It was familiar, yet different. The scent was intoxicating and I found myself breathing deeper with each breath. The fragrance was alluring in a hypnotic sort of way. I pressed my tongue to the back of my teeth as saliva filled my mouth. Swallowing softly, I looked up at him feeling somewhat dazed.

Dark brown hair fell across his radiant blue eyes. They were wide and earnest, like the only thing of beauty he'd ever seen was standing right in front of him. His pale pink lips were curved just right and slightly parted. His cheeks were perfectly smooth. The tension in his body made his muscular frame curve with the divine subtly in all the right places. He was beautiful.

His blue eyes darted to the side, and then back to my face. His brow creased as he leaned a bit closer and asked, "Did you hear me?" Another second passed and he asked, "Ivy?" I looked into his face, neither smiling nor frowning. Just looking. His dark brows pinched together as he gazed over my shoulder and then back at my eyes. He tilted his head forward and repeated himself, "Do you understand? The blood I gave you should have lost its effect a long time ago. You needed it to survive—it healed you. I'd never hurt you, Ivy. Believe me. Remember. Remember the fights we had following that night. If you were smitten with bloodlust and I wanted to use you—I could have." He pressed his lips together waiting for me to respond.

His words washed over me. I knew their meaning was important, but it didn't register with him standing there. Not with him so close. My legs felt like lead. I mentally yanked at them until they could move. When I felt my knee bend, I stepped back from Collin, and nodded. I had to force out the words because my jaw didn't want to move. I was still high on his scent. That had to be what filled my head with every breath I took. It made me want him more than anything I've ever wanted in my entire life. And I couldn't tell him. I couldn't offer the forgiveness. I couldn't offer the kiss. I had to replace the thoughts that floated through my mind with something else—something cold and unforgiving. It was the only way.

My jaw felt like it was made of rusty iron, not wanting to move, not wanting to speak what I had to say. The expression on my face remained vacant, as my gaze was cast toward the floor. "I heard you," I said. It was barely a whisper. With a shallow breath, I dared a glance at his eyes. There was no comprehension in the blue depths. He didn't understand why I wanted him to leave, and I couldn't tell him. His lips parted to speak, but I cut him off, "Just go."

Collin's expression remained the same. He looked down at me perplexed. I could sense his dismay, as I knew he could sense my fear. It didn't matter how hard I tried to bury it, the feelings were jammed into every inch of me. One touch, that's all it would take to shatter me. Then I'd press my lips to his and… The thought cracked like a piece of ice, splintering into tiny shards. He'd hear me. I couldn't think it. I had to force him to leave. Wrapping my arms around myself, I took another step back and he didn't follow. He didn't move forward to close the space between us.

Instead I felt a stony coldness flow through the bond. When I looked up he had stepped away from me. His lips were pressed together. His arms were still folded over his chest with the muscles corded tight as if they could snap at any second. I swallowed the lump in my throat.

As his foot slid away another step, he asked, "Are you still going after the Satan's Stone?" Turning toward him, I gazed into his face for a moment and nodded. He cut eye contact, as his gaze slid off my face and onto the wall. The tension in his stance didn't shift. It didn't change. "You're not going to try to use Eric again, are you?" My mouth went dry. I needed Eric to find the stone. I needed the stone to live. I needed the stone to kill Kreturus. Collin saw the answer before I had a chance to speak. He stepped towards me urgently, "You can't be serious. You can't get what you need from him. He's a rogue. Eric won't do what you expect, Ivy. And next time… " he stepped closer to me, looking down into my eyes with a remorseful expression, "he'll kill you. Al was a warning. He manipulated us."

I could barely think. There was something Lorren had said about Eric, but the words were too far away, lost in the back of mind. I couldn't pull them to my lips. I couldn't tell Collin why Eric had to help me. I couldn't tell him that an angel handpicked the boy and I screwed him up. The words were lost, drifting away into the recesses of my mind. But Collin's gaze didn't turn away. He continued to stare at me with no comprehension on his face.

I pressed my lips together, and said, "There are very few choices then. I die if I approach him. I die if I don't." My heart quickened wondering if he would sense the lie. I didn't have to approach Eric to help me. Eric wasn't the only person who could save me. There was one other way to save me. One other means of removing the sapphire serum lodged in my chest, but I'd never tell him.

Collin's jaw twitched. He opened his mouth and then snapped it shut. Turning on his heel, he ran his fingers through his hair, half pulling half pushing it out of his face. When he turned back to me his eyes flickered like twin blue flames. "I'm not losing you. Not after all this." He sounded like he was talking to himself more than to me. He took a quick step away and I thought he was going to leave, but he turned suddenly.

I sucked in a gasp as he stood less than an inch from my face. He towered over me. The tension in his neck made the muscles throb under his skin. His gaze caught mine. His midnight blue eyes had a ring of fire surrounding them. "There has to be another way to heal you. Some other way to do it without that stone, and without his help."

The words shot out of my mouth like bullets, "There's not!" I replied. "This is the only way. If you try to stop me, you'll kill me. You might as well do it now and save me the agony." My brow pinched together as I looked up into his face, hardly aware of the words I'd said. I hadn't meant to say them.

Collin laughed, "That's the last thing I want. I'll find another way." He paused, his tone softened, "And if there isn't one, I'll track him down myself. Don't do this alone. Ivy, please… "

His hand rose as if he was going to touch my face, but I jerked away. Panic laced my thoughts and spurred my feet into motion. I stumbled backwards nearly losing my footing. The feelings in the pit of my stomach were intensifying the entire time he spoke. Trying to control myself, I breathed slowly, intentionally, as he spoke. My hands turned to fists to keep myself from reaching for him. Every inch of my body wanted to feel him pressed against me. I couldn't maintain the distance much longer, but I didn't have to. Collin watched me. He looked at me as if he'd never seen me before.

Ivy, the thought brushed against my mind.

Icy terror poured down my spine. He was in my mind. I croaked a sound and stepped backwards, pressing my hands to my head as if I were in pain. Collin remained where he was, watching me withdraw from him. When I looked up at his face, the crimson ring was gone.

Finally, he turned to leave. Just as he reached the door, he stopped and turned back to me and said, "He won't touch you. If you go after him, I'll know. And I'll be there." Collin reached for the door and left without another word.

CHAPTER TEN

I wanted to kill Lorren. My body was strung as tight as it could go. My voice came out in rapid squeaks as I yelled at no one and punched the metal support beam in the center of the warehouse. Apryl should have been back already, but she wasn't. My hand balled into a fist and I crushed it again. The sting of cold metal meeting warm flesh abated my anger. As I crashed my hand into it again, I felt the jolt of the impact travel up my arm and into my shoulder. Shaking out my fist, I turned back to the door.

Apryl was standing there, though I didn't see her enter. She wore a wool dress with a pair of black boots that came up to her thighs. Dark hair fell down her back in a shiny sheet. Was Kreturus controlling her? There was no way to know. An eyebrow arched as Apryl walked toward me, throwing down a brown paper bag onto the floor. It tilted sideways and the contents spilled onto the floor. Apryl ignored the bag and continued to walk toward me with a strange expression on her face.

When she was a couple of steps away, I turned sharply. "What?" I growled.

Apryl stopped and shook her head. "Look at your hands. They're covered in blood. And that one looks broken." I gazed at my fists. My hands were still balled tightly, and she was right. They were bright red and slick. Streamers of blood wrapped around my wrists and dripped onto the floor. My left hand had a bone poking through the skin. I opened my hands, flexing the muscles. Apryl sighed and walked back toward the bag and grabbed a bottle of water. She twisted the cap off and turned back to me. As she walked, she scolded, "You can't beat the shit out of poles. If Kreturus showed up now… "

My hands bunched back into fists as I growled, "If he showed up now, I'd kill him." The anger wasn't spent. I could still feel it in muscles, burning with a bright ferocity that was difficult to suppress.

Apryl paused for a moment and then stepped toward me. She gestured for me to extend my hands and poured the water over them. The blood turned pink and spilled to the pavement in a splatter, and splashed onto my bare feet. She turned away and grabbed paper towels and tossed them to me. "Here. Clean up. I got you some shoes too." She tossed them at me. It was a pair of black Chucks. I nodded thanks, cleaned up and slid the shoes onto my cold feet. "It's not anger, ya know."

Her words made my head jerk up as I tied the second shoe. "Then what is it?"

She walked over to where I sat. The wet, bloodstained cement was in front of us. She pushed the brown paper bag toward me. It scraped across the pavement making a noise that made my skin crawl. I peered inside. There were snacks and a tray of Chinese food. The tray had condensation sticking to the lid. It was still hot. I picked it up and ate as she spoke.

"Thought you'd be hungry. Didn't know what you'd want, so there's a bunch of stuff in there." I nodded thanks, and she continued. "Anger is something that you can control. But that burning intensity that feels like anger, it's really something else. Only the strong have it, and even very few of them get it. I thought it had to do with age, or the demon that made you. You know, the older the Valefar, the purer the content of demon blood. That in turn would make a stronger Valefar… but with you," she arched her eyebrow, "I'm not so sure."

I shoved a piece of broccoli in my mouth. "If it's not anger, what is it? You still didn't tell me."

She hesitated. "I didn't tell you, because it may not be the same for you. If you really are a half-breed," I looked up at her unamused, and she smiled sheepishly, "or whatever you want to call it—then it might affect you differently. Anger is an emotion—it's a reaction to a stimulus that upset you. Anger is a defense mechanism, and helps your body prepare to fight. Well, demon blood works in a similar way. It's called *Akayleah*. It's like anger in that it manifests in response to a stimulus, but it's unlike anger in that you cannot control it."

Her words strung questions together in my head. I put down the tray of food and grabbed a can of Coke. As I pressed the metal tab the can hissed opened. "But everyone is telling me that I can control it. They also thought it was anger." I shook my head. "This doesn't make sense, Apryl."

Her eyebrows shot up as her shoulders shot back. Her jaw hung open for a spilt second before she spoke. Her voice was defensive. "I'm not lying to you. Why would I? You're the only person who can free me from this shitty life." Apryl's spine resumed its former slump as she leaned forward and stabbed a piece of broccoli.

"I don't know who you're talking to, or why they didn't know. It's not like it's common knowledge. This isn't basic Valefar stuff. It's stuff I learned from being at the Pool of Lost Souls. Every demon has blood. Its power is from age and acquisition." She laughed, "Acquisition, that's the nice way of saying they viciously took the power from someone else, and then, that person died horrifically as a result.

"Anyway, the power makes the demon. The demon made the Valefar with their blood. You should know that part." When she looked at me I nodded. Some of it was new, but I knew most of it. "*Akayleah* is a demon ability. It's kind of like an emotion, but it's not. Something has to cause it to occur, and when it does—then there's no stopping it. Imagine being so angry that you go into an insane rage. Imagine it contorts your mind, your body, and every bit of your appearance. That's what *Akayleah* is. It's when your blood overtakes your mind, and you have the compulsion to act without thought. The more powerful the demon, the more severe the *Akayleah*."

My jaw dropped open while she was speaking. My wrists went limp, dropping the piece of food that was skewered on my fork. The piece of chicken slid onto the floor, and I didn't move. It felt like all the air was sucked out of the room. I stared unblinking for a moment, utterly shocked.

"Why didn't they know?" I asked. "How is that possible? The angels think they know everything about the demons. They made it sound like the war was all but won—until I came along. But that can't be. Not if stuff like this is possible, and they didn't even know about it." I paused, thinking of the ramifications for me, "*Akayleah* destroys the demon's mind? Their body? Everything?" I asked, horrified.

She nodded, "From what I understand, it does. But Ivy, I barely know about this and I shouldn't. I'm a nobody. I don't have enough demon power to effonate, never mind have issues with *Akayleah*… but, maybe you do." I pressed my hands to my face, and rubbed hard, pushing my hair back. Apryl watched me. "Once *Akayleah* starts, you can't stop it."

Looking at the floor, I pressed my eyes together. "It's already started." My voice was flat and listless. "It started in a battle last year. My anger got away from me. I felt insane. I killed so many Valefar and I felt absolutely nothing. Their deaths didn't plague me later. Their cries of agony didn't haunt me in any way." Taking a deep breath, I sighed and looked at my sister—my Valefar sister who I would have killed with the rest, without a second glance, if she stood in front of me that night. "Why don't the angels know about *Akayleah*?"

"The demons hide it," she said. "They hide it like it's their most precious treasure." My face contorted with disgust. Apryl leaned forward, "Think about it, Ivy. The Angel Demon wars have gone on for eons, but the demons have a weapon that can only make them stronger and more powerful. And since it's so rare, they think it's a treasure. Each demon's highest hope is that his blood will be powerful enough to evoke a ruthless *Akayleah* when the time comes. Your creator must have been very powerful. Either that or the demon blood did something weird to the angel blood when you were changed."

I nodded, not knowing what to say. Somehow the angels hadn't heard of any of this. It was like hiding a weapon the size of a football field under a tablecloth. Demons had this ability and the angels knew nothing about it. And worst of all, I had this ability as well. Turning to Apryl I asked, "How do I keep from awaking it?"

She looked at me and shrugged. "I don't know. It sounds like you already have. Maybe your angel blood is holding it in check. Maybe it isn't, but either way caving in and allowing your emotions to dictate your actions is stupid. You're allowing something else, something strong, to overtake you. Allowing anything to do that to you can force your *Akayleah* into action." She paused, her eyes raking over my hair, my face, and my forearms that were healed and seamless once again. "If you're already having issues with your *Akayleah*, why isn't it apparent? I should be able to see something, and not just when it's invoked. It should have left a scar." Her eyes narrowed a bit as they slid over my face and arms again. "The scars are revered in the Underworld. They would protect you from other demons, lesser demons—but you have none." She locked my gaze. Her green eyes suspicious. "Why?"

Glancing at her out of the corner of my eye, I leaned back on my hands. My injuries had healed although my skin where the bone poked through would remain pink for several hours. Swallowing, I wondered what I should say. My gut clenched tightly when I thought of telling her about Lorren, so I said, "I healed it. I didn't know what it was, so I scraped it off. Scales appeared on my face and shoulders. I cut them off, and regular skin replaced them when I healed." I laughed nervously, as if I were laughing at myself. "I thought I was turning into a demon."

"You were." Apryl's green eyes were completely serious. "And don't remove them again. They could save you in the future."

CHAPTER ELEVEN

Sleep tugged at me, sucking me into the black abyss again. It felt more like a vision than a dream, and maybe it was. I was getting so confused as to what was sleep and what wasn't. The darkness faded into a dull gray mist, and then I was standing alone staring at something. At first I thought it was a patch of darkness where the light refused to shine. There were places like that in Hell, places where the shadows seemed alive and malicious. The patch of darkness shifted and swirled like bubbles on top of boiling water.

When they cleared I was standing before a mirror made of black glass. It was more substantial than the last time I saw it. Collin's words echoed somewhere in the back of my mind. His voice whispered a warning that I couldn't hear. Stepping towards it, I felt curiosity ignite inside of me. It was so strange. The mirror shone like glass, but instead of showing a reflection, there was nothing. It made no sense. I slid my foot towards it, closer, closer, closer until I was nearly touching the glass. The frigid mirror showed no reflection still, but as I gazed into its depths, I thought I could see something. It was small and silvery. Maybe it was a candlestick? Or something similar, but it looked so distant that I couldn't be certain.

I pressed my hand to the mirror expecting to be met with chilled glass, but my hand slipped through the plane. It was no thicker than a layer of skin, and my hand sunk straight through into its warm depths. Panic raced through me. Startled, I pulled my hand back. It came free from the mirror. I bent the fingers, counting them, examining that they were intact and unchanged. Each slender finger bent and the skin was still pale and smooth. I examined the back of my hand and then flipped it over and looked at my palm. Nothing had changed. The black glass seemed to have no effect.

Eyes wide, I looked up at the glass and saw someone standing on the other side. A shriek ripped from my lips as I stumbled backwards. There was a woman in the glass! She was clad in a black gown that covered her from neck to toe. A black cloak hung around her shoulders with the hood pulled up, obscuring her face.

I snapped my mouth shut, and swallowed hard, examining the woman in the glass. A memory. A thought swirled at the back of my mind, whispering, *Danger. Destruction. Death.* My palms were covered in cold sweat. My foot slid away from the dark mirror.

The movement seemed to startle her, because her head tilted up and she saw me. Her mouth first formed a small O, and then melted into a smile that tugged the corners of her mouth. Her lips parted as if she were going to speak. She took a step toward me. I could see nothing but eyes the color of amethyst with large pupils black as night.

"How utterly delightful." Her voice was deep, and dripping with scorn. I wanted to turn and walk away, but power flowed from the glass. I could feel it reaching out and snaking into the place I stood, holding me still. I stood motionless as her ruthless eyes washed over me. "This is the one to defeat Kreturus?" She chortled one short burst of laughter. "You are no more than a child. And a child that doesn't know who she is, at that. Come closer girl." Without meaning to, my foot slid up to the edge of the black glass. "Are you the one who awakened me? Are you the one who shoved a girl through the glass? And are you the one who just slid an arm through into my home?" I nodded, too stunned to reply. The hooded figure stood silently watching me for a moment. Her head tilted as her arms folded and a gloved hand extended a single finger to touch the side of her shadowed face. "Mmmm. Then, it is time." Her voice contained power. "Come."

The word rang like crystal. My ears resonated with her voice. Before I realized what was happening, my foot glided forward through the glass like something was pulling on it. My right arm reached out slowly as I fought for control of my body. The woman in the hood laughed as I battled with myself to defy her command and remain on this side of the mirror. However, my other foot began to slide forward. It was like pushing two drops of water together. At some point they are drawn to one another and cannot pull back. I was one drop. The woman in the black hood was the other. The whispers in my mind wouldn't be silenced. It was Collin's warning that rang the loudest, warning me, trying to save me. *Stay on this side of the mirror.* Once I passed through, I would never be the same.

But it was too late. Both feet were sucked into the black glass, followed by the rest of me. As I passed through the mirror, it clung to me like tape. Every part of my body was sticking and sliding at the same time. The mirror was nothing as it seemed the last time I saw it. Last time it was an inanimate object, just sitting there. It showed things like a mirror should. There was power inside the glass. And there was a simple reason why the glass contained power. When I emerged on the other side, the hooded figure stood with her arms folded. She was tall and thin. The black cloak hid her slender figure. Her cowl obscured her face.

She watched me as I gazed across the room made of gray slate and granite. Every surface was smooth and cold, made of slick stone. Water poured down a wall in front of me over pieces of broken boulders. Where the water began, I didn't know. It was too high up to see. It cascaded like a small waterfall behind a massive table with two chairs. A large flame radiated heat and light from the center of the room. It clung high to the ceiling, suspended in air, and remained there without burning anything it touched. Polished granite was slick under my feet. A chaise made from stone was at the opposite end of the room. There was nothing soft in this space. There was no cloth, no linens, no drapes, no fabric save for what the woman wore on her back.

The hooded figure moved toward the stone table and sat, gesturing for me to follow. I sat opposite her. My jaw had locked and I could feel the muscles twitching. I tried to relax. But I couldn't. Not here. Not with her.

My voice was certain as I spoke, "You're the Demon Princess—the one who failed to kill Kreturus, and was banished to the black mirror and... destroyed."

She responded by forming a smile with her thin red lips. "Yes, I am. And I survived. I did not fail, little one. I have bided my time, and my time has come."

CHAPTER TWELVE

I opened my mouth to speak, but before I could utter a word my chest tightened. It felt like a vice-like grip was crushing the air out of my lungs. A rush of wind escaped over my lips. It sparkled like winter snow as it rose from my mouth and traveled across the table. The shimmering breath hovered in front of her, before she inhaled deeply. Her crimson lips parted and my glittering breath vanished inside her mouth.

The vice released me, and I fell forward onto the table. My head hit the stone before I could stop it. I'd been pulling so hard against her that I didn't stop when she released me. A smile twisted as she watched a trail of blood streak down into my eye. Excitement forced her to her feet.

This time I didn't wait. I didn't sit down like a nice girl and wait to see what she would say. Instead, I shot out of the chair and pulled my comb. My violet mark shimmered on my brow. I touched the Celestial Silver to my mark. The tines extended in an instant. The Demon Princess stopped before she reached me, hissing at the blade.

"What did you do to me?" I shouted. It felt as if she'd taken something from me—something of substance that was pressing on me. Now that it was gone, I could sense its absence.

She slid back, away from the end of the blades. "I did you a favor—a favor given freely—and this is how you repay me?" Her hands were at her sides, though tension remained in her shoulders. She was ready to fight.

"What did you take from me? I can feel it!" Worry ripped through me. I couldn't fight her. She was supposed to be dead! The most powerful demon in Hell put her here and broke the mirror that held her. And yet, here I was. And there she stood—very much alive.

"Look at your chest. Look for the poison that threatened you more than I ever did. It was a weight crushing you, stealing your power, and hiding your talent. Look at it." Her hood nodded once. Gleaming violet eyes were radiant. Her arms folded across her chest. Her billowing sleeves fell back, but the gloves she wore covered her entire arm. I could see nothing of her flesh.

Part of me thought that it could be a trap. Her words made me uneasy. But, I felt the lack of something, something that had been substantial. I couldn't allow myself to hope that the poison was gone. I pulled back my neckline with my left hand, not dropping my weapon. When I stole a glance at my marred skin, I saw nothing. No blue vein. No scar. No nothing. The poison appeared to be gone. Even Lorren couldn't do that. My throat tightened at the thought.

Straightening my spine, I dropped my hand and backed away from her. "What was the price? There are no gifts freely given. Not from your kind."

The Demon Princess laughed softly and returned to the table. She slid onto the stone seat again and surveyed me over her fingers, as she pressed them together. "There is no price, little one. The poison is still there. It will still kill you." My mouth opened, but I snapped it shut again when she shot me a sharp glance. "I did more for you in that one action than anyone has ever done for you in your entire life. The fool who froze the serum was still allowing its venom to poison you." I slid down in my chair, looking at nothing. Her words surrounded me, until I felt like I was drowning. "Sloppy work for an angel. He could have healed you, but he didn't." Her eyebrow arched. "How curious. And was this angel friend or foe?" She leaned backward slightly, resting against the back of the stone chair.

Apprehension laced my thoughts. This seemed like a dream, but I knew it wasn't. It was like a living vision. This demon pulled me from my dreams and into her world. I was trapped. Curiosity got the better of me and I asked, "How'd you know it was an angel? And what did you do? It doesn't feel the same."

She tilted her head and leaned forward. Her black gloved fingers tapped twice, "Residue. Angel residue leaves a… taste." Her nose crinkled as she said the word. "I took that from you, so I could fix it. He left the venom crystalized, so that you could not use your demonic abilities without it costing you. He was very clever. It was well masked. But I am too old and too powerful to be fooled so easily. I have not healed you, nor will I. The poison is there by your own hand and none but you can take it away." She rose from her chair and walked towards me slowly. Her eyes slid over my body as I leaned on the table.

I clutched my weapon so tightly in my hand that my knuckles were turning white. I didn't turn. I looked straight ahead wondering what the hell Lorren was doing. He didn't seem like he was helping me at all. Yet, he was protecting Eric. That made no sense.

When she said I could heal myself, I laughed at her words. The sound was hollow and callused, "I can take it away?" I looked up at her, and she nodded. I could see nothing of her face, but I didn't have to know that she was lying. I answered, "I would have, if it were possible."

She laughed, "Foolish girl. You cannot put anyone higher than yourself, lest you die. When you destroy Kreturus, you can put everything the way you want it, but until then—you will waste away. The venom will slowly kill you from within—unless you remove it yourself. There is no stopping venom any other way, no matter what that angel told you. He limited your abilities by freezing the sapphire serum and nothing more."

I flexed my hands and loosened my grip on my comb. The flick of her gaze said she noticed the movement, no matter how tiny it was. She stood in front of me, black gown billowing around her ankles. The light from the false sun above hid her face in complete darkness.

"Why did you call me here?" I turned my head to look up at her. "Why did you pull me through the glass?" I rose in my chair, stood, and looked her in the eye.

"To teach you to use your power," she replied. "What other reason could there possibly be?" She tilted her head back as her red lips pulled into a tight smile. Silence passed between us.

There was no way for me to defeat Kreturus without using all of my abilities. It was something that I could feel in my bones. I just knew it to be true. But, learning from her—it made my gut twist into knots. Collin warned me not to use my powers, but I knew I would have to if I wanted to defeat Kreturus.

My eyes narrowed to slits as I took a step closer to her. "Why would you help me?"

"I believe it is exceedingly expected for demons to be vindictive and hell-bent on revenge." She pressed the fingertips of her black gloves together and turned. Her gown flowed as she moved. When she turned to sit, the skirt swirled slightly higher than her ankle. Before the gauzy fabric fell back into place, I saw pale human skin on her leg above her boot. My eyes flicked back to her face before she saw me. She was human. The Demon Princess didn't notice the flick of my eye. She looked up at me from her seat. "The question is… are you willing to learn?"

I leaned across the table, staring at her. This woman came looking for me. This Demon Princess that was supposed to be dead sucked me into this place for one reason—to kill Kreturus. It made an akward alliance. I didn't see myself siding with a demon, but a scorned demon was better than winging it. She wanted to teach me, and I needed to learn. One concern rose to the top of my mind—if I killed Kreturus, and this woman's dark powers exceeded my own—how could I keep her from killing me? She wanted Kreturus' throne. If I won, what was keeping her from killing me and taking it? A plan formed haphazardly in my mind. I was a few inches from her shrouded face. "No," I breathed, and she flinched. "The question is will you teach me everything you know. Will you teach it to me fully? Will you teach me so I cannot fail?" I leaned back, sliding into my seat. I swallowed hard, knowing the road I was about to choose had a steep price, and once chosen— there was no going back. That was the only thing I could think of that would keep her from trying to kill me later. She was powerful and somehow she outsmarted Kreturus, and survived his wrath.

The Demon Princess placed her gloved hands on the table in front of her. She leaned forward and smiled wide, revealing pointed eyeteeth behind her red lips. "Do I sense a bargain, young Ivy Taylor?" Her words were light and playful.

I leaned back in my chair, draping my arm over the back. "Yes, you do." This was the most powerful demon there ever was, next to Kreturus. If I had her skills with my power, I could beat him. I could win. I'd survive. But I had to get her to agree to teach me, and demons had a way of withholding things. A bargain would force her to divulge the stores of her knowledge, all of them. "Teach me everything you know, without exception."

Her hands folded in front of her in an attempt to hide her excitement. "And what would my payment be?"

Tension ran down my spine, and raced up the muscles in my arms. "What do you want?"

"In addition to killing Kreturus?" she asked leaning forward in her chair.

I nodded. "Yes. You said you'd teach me how to use my power to kill him without a bargain. What payment do you want for teaching me everything you know?" I tilted my head, gauging the princess. She would ask for something else, something big.

Her lips were smooth and in a perfectly straight line. "Bring me an angel."

My eyebrow twitched. "An angel? What for?" I leaned forward, trying to hide my shock. My disdain.

"It's not your concern. You asked what would be worth bargaining for. I could teach you enough to kill Kreturus without teaching you everything. If I allow you to overpower me, there must be a price. The price is angel blood from a living, breathing angel." She leaned back in her chair; her hands remained on the table in front of her. Several minutes passed when she finally said, "If you are unwilling, then… "

Something she said caught my attention, "I'm not unwilling. How do I know? How do I know that the things you teach me will be worth the price? How can I believe you have the power that I need to overpower him, when you failed to do it yourself? He defeated you. I'm taking lessons from the loser, and paying through the eyes for it."

My words were too careless, the tone of my voice too flippant. Before I could blink, she flew across the table. My chair was knocked out from under me as we flew backwards with her forearm pressing against my throat. When my back slammed into the wall, she leaned closer to my face growling, "Because I was a careless, stupid girl. My arrogance cost me my crown. But he did not destroy me as he intended. I was stronger than he suspected—and you will be too, if you don't make the same stupid mistakes." I tried to suck in air as she spoke, but there was too much weight on my throat. She released me and I slid down the wall into a puddle on the floor. I wanted to jump up and attack her, but instead, I rose slowly, controlling my twitching muscles. She turned and looked over her shoulder and a sense of familiarity washed over me. I thought it was from my dreams, but I wasn't so sure. "The price is an angel—a living angel. You will bring him to me after you defeat Kreturus."

Swallowing hard, I looked at her. This was crossing a line. Once I stepped over it, there was no way back. A bargain with a demon was permanent—binding. Once I entered into the agreement, it could not be undone. "You're certain that sapphire serum won't affect me until Kreturus is dead? The venom won't kill me first?"

She nodded once. "Yes. But remember this. A bargain is a bargain. There is no way to alter the terms. There is no escape once your blood is given. It's more binding than an oath. Failure to complete the bargain has dire consequences for both of us. You would kill the Demon King and steal his throne. You would have more power than me. There would be no one to stop you." She watched me as she spoke, her words slowly lulling me into thinking this was a good plan.

If I accepted the bargain, it would change me. But, I'd already changed so much. I just wanted to survive. I wanted this to end. There'd been so many things I wanted to do—wanted to be. Now all that was gone. My life was gone. This is what remained. I had the chance to kill the Demon King, and I knew she could teach me. I had the power. The hush murmurs were all around me. They knew I had power, but they also knew that I had no idea how to use it. I already demonstrated that time and time again. I wanted the certainty that this agreement would bring. I stared at her. Her arms were poised on the table. A gloved finger pressed into the stone. That was the only thing that told me that she cared about my answer. She wanted this. The angel she wanted was important, but I didn't know how or why. And I had no idea how I was supposed to bring her a living angel. It didn't matter. There was no other choice. I thrust out my hand, "You have a bargain."

She reached for my wrist, and a black blade appeared in her hand. She sliced it across my palm in a swift motion, causing blood to pour out of the cut. I flinched as the blade tore apart my skin, and my mouth opened to ask what she was doing. Before I could speak, she sliced her own palm. With a quick movement she gripped our bloodied palms together and there was a loud crack overhead. I winced, and tried to pull my hand back to retreat. It sounded like the ceiling would cave in.

A black chalice appeared, catching the blood that flooded from our hands. When Locoicia reached for the cup, she swirled the contents. Two swirls of blood intertwined on top of the dark liquid. She grinned widely revealing her eye teeth, and set the object high on a shelf with several other gilded cups.

A wide smile snaked across her lips. "It is done. There is no such thing as a bloodless bargain. The chalice holds the bargain, and will dictate when it is completed and if either of us defaults on our end of the deal. Punishment for abandoning this bargain will be a prompt demise. How interesting…" Her violet eyes glimmered like precious stones.

My throat constricted like she'd kicked my neck. "I didn't consent to that!" My hand tightened around hers. "The bargain was your teachings in exchange for an angel. That was it!"

She shook her head as she laughed. "The blood made the bargain, not me. Look at the liquid that appeared in the cup. I've seen many substances appear to bind the bargain. It provides a little insight as to what might occur if we abandon the agreement. Once a blood bargain is made, it cannot be broken." She reached for the black goblet and thrust it into my hands. I looked down at the swirling contents. The liquid was thick and dark—completely opaque. I couldn't see the bottom of the cup. There might as well have been tar sitting under the blood. Locoicia spoke, as she removed the glass from my hand. "It's black as night, and viscous. Thick. That only means one thing— there is no way to escape a bargain of this magnitude with a slap on the wrist. No, liquid this thick and dark only has one repercussion—death."

CHAPTER THIRTEEN

The musty scent of the warehouse filled my senses. Before I knew what happened, I peeled my eyes open and looked around. Sunlight was pouring through holes in the metal exterior. I sat up slowly, and clutched my hand to my chest. Breathing hard, I tried to calm down. Apryl was sitting across the room on a pile of crates watching me. When I said nothing, her attention went back to a magazine she had on her lap.

I rubbed my eyes and pushed my hair out of my face, and took a deep steadying breath. It wasn't real. It was a vision. Or a dream. I shook my head, trying to dislodge the thoughts. Pulling a ponytail holder from my wrist, I yanked my hair back, and wrapped the narrow piece of elastic around several times to hold my hair in place. As I rubbed my face once more, I dropped my hands to my lap. That's when I saw it. There was a pink jagged line across my right palm—exactly where the Demon Princess sliced.

I screamed.

The sound of my voice cut through the empty space and echoed back in my face. Apryl jumped off the crates and was next to me in seconds. "What?" she asked. "What happened?" She crouched next to me, trying to fathom what had spooked me. She looked back at my face, but I didn't look at her.

I couldn't look at her. Oh my God. What did I do? It couldn't have been real. Yanking down my shirt, I pulled my neckline until I could see the scar. Smooth pale skin. Nothing else. No blue line marring my breast. No mark of venom trickling through my body and slowly killing me. As my heart thumped in my chest, it felt like the world stopped turning. Everything was sliding away in one slow motion. There was no gravity, no feeling of safety. Nothing was taken for granted. Life itself was never a promise. And my life, the life I knew, the one I'd been fighting for—it was over.

All the things I'd done, all the chances I took, and the lives I risked—it was all for nothing. There would be no going back to school. No dates. No prom. No normal, not anymore. I sucked in a ragged breath trying to wrap my mind around it. Lorren had lied to me. An angel lied to me! How was that even possible? Locoicia, the Demon Princess, said he could have healed me and didn't. Lorren said the only way to do it was to get my soul back from Collin first. But he lied. The Demon Princess said he lied.

And I struck up a blood bargain with her. Of course, I did. It made perfect sense. It sounded totally rational in my mind when I did it, but now, now in the light of day—it was insane! I took the word of a demon over the word of an angel.

I jumped up. Apryl watched me. The expressions shifting across my face had started rather calmly compared to what I was feeling now. I clutched my head, "This can't be happening. It can't be. I never left, right?" I turned sharply to Apryl who stood behind me, not knowing what to do or what was wrong.

She shook her head. "No, you didn't leave. What's the matter?" I didn't answer her. I couldn't say it. I couldn't admit it. I continued to pace until she stepped in front of me. Her green eyes were wide like two big green dinner plates. "Stop." She put her hands on my shoulders. I froze and looked at her. "What happened?"

My jaw opened and I meant to speak, but nothing came out. The words, blood bargain rang in my mind. The sound of my heart pumping seemed so loud. Apryl didn't release me, so I stood there until words formed.

My mouth felt stiff, like it was made of wood. My lips wouldn't form words, they couldn't. But Apryl wouldn't let go, and I didn't want her to. I wanted my sister. I wanted my life back.

Swallowing hard, I told her. "While I slept, I had a vision. And... I made a blood bargain with a demon." I pressed my lips together, fearful to say more. Apryl's mouth dropped open as her grip on my shoulders slipped. She took a step back. Her horror only made it worse. I added, "I had to. There was no other choice... There never is."

I folded my arms over my chest and pulled them tightly to my body. I never thought my inability to call light would lead to something like this. I shook my head, knowing that wasn't true. That wasn't what made the blood bargain—it was me. I did it. Willingly. I pressed the palms of my hands to my face and rubbed, as I walked away from Apryl.

"What do you owe the demon?" she asked hesitantly. I couldn't bear to look at her. She might not remember me, but I remembered her. The lines carved between her crinkled brow deepened as she waited for my answer. Her fingers twitched subtly at her sides.

My eyes cut to her worried face. There was no denying it. I had to tell her. "An angel. I promised a payment of a living angel. And if I default, I die."

Apryl's mouth opened in horror. "Do you know what you did? Do you know what you offered?" She smacked me with two hands, in rapid succession, one after the other on either side of my head. I didn't block her smacks. She leaned into my downturned face, asking, "How the hell are you going to bring an angel to the Underworld? That demon set you up. You will default on that bargain. There is no way to get an angel into the demon realm alive! You can't put a bow on him, and drop him off at the demon's doorstep. The demon asked for a payment you couldn't possibly provide. What the hell were you thinking?" She slapped me again, but this time I grabbed her hand. Glaring at her, my hand tightened around her wrist. She shook with anger as she hissed, "You gave your crown to someone else. You made a bargain you cannot keep." I released her hand and it fell to her side like a piece of dead wood.

She turned from me, and wrapped her arms around her middle. It was something our mother did when she was worried. She'd walk a few steps, turn, and repeat—all while keeping her arms folded snugly across her body. We both had the same mannerism. I nearly choked as I watched her. My mother would have... I shook my head, dislodging the thought. I had no idea what my mother would have done. Both of her daughters had demon blood flowing through their veins. That was different than any life she would have imagined for us. I blinked away the thoughts.

Something Apryl said made me pause. I spoke quickly, sensing she was ready to walk away from me. "Why can't an angel enter Hell? They took it over during one of the wars. They were down there once before, right?" Lorren was down there. He was an angel, right? That was why I thought I could bring one to the Demon Princess. Because of him.

She looked over her shoulder at me. Her eyes were glassy. Apryl's lips turned into a thin line as she fought to control her emotions. She laughed softly, "You don't understand." She turned towards me, arms still folded across her chest. "When you kill Kreturus there would have been peace. You had no intention of attacking the angels. But not now," she shook as she spoke. "Now you will drag an offering to the demon who helped you. That's clearly an attack. And they will reciprocate if you force one of their kind down there. The Guardian was left there so the angels could leave. Their kind doesn't take well to the Underworld. It… Affects them oddly.

"Ivy, if you fail to complete your bargain, then you'll die. That demon that struck the bargain with you, will steal your crown, and I have no doubt that an angel attack would follow. The angels would never see it coming. They would have had peace with you, but then you die when the blood bargain takes effect. There will be war no matter what you do. There will never be peace. There will never be rest."

Her jaw hung open, as her chest constricted. She looked up at me with her eyes creased in the corners, "I will never be free. I will never die, because the Valefar will not be released." I opened my mouth to speak, but she cut me off. "No! You listen and you listen well. You had no more time for mistakes. There were no more chances to waste." She shook her head, looking at me with complete disgust. "You could have walked away. You could have said no. A blood bargain is willingly entered into by both sides. You *chose* this." She shook her head, making her dark auburn hair brush against her cheek, and turned away.

I watched her leave without calling after her. As Apryl pulled open the door the morning sun drenched her in golden light. Her dark hair looked like it was on fire, as she hesitated in the doorway. She stood there for a moment. My breath caught in my throat. Apryl didn't act like a Valefar. She wasn't full of vengeance like Eric. She wasn't deceitful like Jake. She seemed to find her own path and stuck to it. The only life she'd known was torn away when the Pool of Lost Souls was attacked. The Guardian was dead for all I knew, just like the sister I'd grown up with. But this Apryl, the one that was walking away scared me. She saw through me, unmasking things fast and furious. She was helpful.

And for some reason, she was on my side—until now—until I did something that was unforgivable. I watched her pause in the doorway, waiting to see if she would look over her shoulder, but she didn't. Apryl took a step forward, and the door closed behind her leaving me alone in the darkness.

CHAPTER THIRTEEN

Days passed. The sun swept across the sky, and sank into the sea every night. But Apryl did not return. Nor did I expect her to. I saw the look on her face. I failed her. She was trapped, and I wasn't the one who could free her. I couldn't even free myself. As time passed, I no longer worried about the Guardian's death. He had to be alive down there, otherwise the world would be overrun with hellish creatures. Since there were no demons running through the streets, I thought we were okay. My visions came and went. They turned into tutorials—lessons on how to harness my dark powers. Locoicia pulled me through every vision, every time. There was no rest. The venom in my chest didn't weaken me as it had, but it still took a toll. And the Demon Princess was irritated if I didn't show my face once a day. She said there was no time. And there wasn't.

Her black cowl covered her face, as always. "Do it again." Her words were cold. The dark gauzy fabric of the gown clung to her, showing off her slender form. Dark gloves lined her slender fingers, resting on top of her folded arms, gently tapping as her eyes cut into me.

The things she was asking me to do weren't innate. The acts weren't something that I wanted to know how to do. I had no desire to learn to do them, but I needed to know. Locoicia said it was necessary, and I bargained to learn *everything*. Everything without exception. As our lessons continued, I realized the insanity of that request. What was even weirder was her willingness to accept the bargain, and teach me. It made me wonder who was crazier. Her? Or me?

I quickly learned that immense power coursed through my veins, and that I could command it with simple words or gestures. The dark magic felt heavy and thick, like hot fudge clinging to my insides. The first time I recognized the sensation, I was shocked to realize exactly how much power I had. It was power that Apryl lacked. It was power that Kreturus wanted. Locoicia explained that demons have limited abilities, as do angels—but me… I was different. I was a hybrid of both races, which gave me more power than all of them. I just had no idea how to use it. It turns out my power manifested during my enraged fits, because I was tapping into the same place within me, calling on the same power source to fuel my burning anger. Apparently, I didn't have to risk turning into a demon to use my power. There was no need to tap into my ability to *Akayleah*. And no reason to tell her I even had that ability. Or that I'd already used it. After all, I never promised to divulge everything.

So, Locoicia taught me. She was impatient, demanding, and expected me to learn things the first time with no questions asked. I didn't like her, which was fine because the feeling was mutual. I could tell. She'd fumed away, trapped in a piece of glass forever, irritated. Meanwhile, I was the one who was going to do what she couldn't—kill the demon king. It wasn't that I was stupid, or a slow learner. I grasped proficiency of her lessons quickly. It was the depth of my mastery that made her fume. We skipped straight from beginner to advanced during the same lesson. And I didn't like the advanced applications. My stomach twisted just thinking about it.

But, she didn't give me time to think. Locoicia's teaching methods were sink or swim. I sputtered along half sinking, until I got it. And when I failed, I felt the brunt of her power.

The lesson she was teaching me wasn't going well. A sharp pain pierced my thoughts and slid down my spine. *Concentrate*, I scolded myself. Locoicia pressed into my mind, forcing me to maintain my focus in order to keep her out. Her attempts to slip into my mind made it difficult to consider what I was doing. The moral implications didn't have time to emerge in my mind. She would mentally berate me as I tried to accomplish the task she gave. I was much stronger than she was, but she was more resourceful and more skilled.

It wasn't her power that made Locoicia dangerous. It was the way in which she used it.

Darkness flowed through me thick and hot until a seam on the forearm of her gown split opened. Locoicia's blood was black as tar and flowed from the wound. I stopped, and the severed skin closed immediately. The Demon Princess smoothed her hand over her torn garment and the threads retied themselves into proper stitches. I did what she wanted. I tore open her arm in one controlled slice.

"And the price?" I asked.

She looked over her shoulder at me. The flesh on her forearms was pale with tiny black spots—demon scales. Was she human or demon? Or a human turned demon from too much *Akayleah*? Locoicia had more power than she let on. She responded promptly, "Pain, of course."

The moment she said it, it felt like my stomach was ripped from my body. In one swift moment the air was stripped away and replaced with searing pain. When the instant passed, I realized I was clutching my gut and had started to turn inward to try to ease to deal with it.

She flicked her wrist, as if she were holding an imaginary whip, and a small red line appeared on my left hand. It stung for half a second before the skin was sliced opened. I winced, and she was next to me in a second hissing in my ear. "I will cover every last bit of you in lashes, if you fail to hide your pain from me again. Pain is weakness." She moved away. "Everyone pays the price. Only the weak acknowledge pain. You will not be weak. You will recognize the pain, but you will not feel it. You will feel nothing. Do you understand?" I nodded. In theory, I understood perfectly. Hide my pain. In practice? Well, that was another issue. She said, "Again."

We worked for hours until I was so tired, I couldn't see straight. She managed to get into my mind more than once. That scared me the most, which almost seems funny. Calling forth dark powers didn't scare me. Slicing open the Demon Princess' skin or scales or whatever she had didn't faze me. But, the thought of her perusing my mind—the thought of her seeing bits of my shattered life was non-negotiable. It made me fight harder to keep her out. I had no idea what she was capable of, but I wouldn't underestimate her. Kreturus did that and look what happened—she was alive and training his assassin.

The lesson shifted. We were learning something else. Locoicia walked next to me, leaning over my shoulder. I was barely able to stand. The lessons did not have a power price, like they did for most. But they still exhausted me. A human body could only endure so much pain. There was a point of no return. If I passed it, if she mis-estimated my pain threshold, I'd die. My body felt stiff, no longer wanting to bend as I moved. I ignored it.

Locoicia insisted that I learn standing up. So I stood, with my feet apart and my hands at my sides. She said, "Reach into your pocket. There will be whatever you need—a key, coin, or gold. Riches are all within your reach, now. Simply do as I say, and extract them." She explained the charm once. There was no repetition in her lessons—no wasted words. If I didn't glean everything from her meager verbiage, she became angry.

Nodding, I did as she said, and reached into my pocket. At first there was nothing there, just the rough cotton lining of the pocket between my fingers. But a different sensation brushed against me, and I felt the paper bills form in my hand. I pulled the money out of my pocket and put it on the table, in front of Locoicia.

That was incredibly easy. I stared at the paper bills, somewhat shocked.

There was no more time to fathom the cash on the table. Or ask if it was real, fake, or where it came from. The pain price hit me half a second later. It felt like I was being cut from neck to navel. The feeling of the knife slicing through skin and muscles, until it stopped in my stomach, was real. Horror washed over me. My hands pressed on my abdomen, frantically searching for the weapon that caused the sensation. My fingers twitched, as I curled forward, cradling my body from the onslaught of pain. The blade, the blade I couldn't see, lodged in my stomach and slid up to my neck leaving a hot stream in its wake. My hands were pressing on me, following the trail of agony up to my throat, but when I pulled my palms away there wasn't a speck of blood on them. Terror made my voice ring out. My hands clutched my stomach, but there was no wound. The pain was completely internal. Unable to bear another moment, I felt my body dry heave. Everything inside me curdled and came out my mouth, and onto the floor.

Locoicia showed no compassion. Gasping for breath, my bare hands clutched the stone beneath my fingers until the spasms that raked my stomach stopped. When I looked up at the hooded figure, her violet eyes were calm. There wasn't an ounce of anger within their depths. Without a word, she crooked her finger, and flicked her wrist. A welt the size of her fist ripped down my spine. My back arched in response, as a cry ripped out of my throat. The pain intensified as I felt a warm trail of blood run down my skin, and stick to my shirt. I bit back a second scream as the sting dug deep into my muscles and more blood spilled from the wound. Failing to remain still, utterly failing not to flinch, my jaw opened and a ragged breath contorted with pain emerged. The sound of my raw scream echoed through the room. Horrified, I clutched my sides, unable to reach my back. Unable to see or feel with my hands what she had done to me. I didn't know if it was real or only in my mind.

My heart beat wildly, as I looked up at the Demon Princess. Blood red lips were pulled into a tight thin line. Indigo eyes were cold and merciless. She stepped toward me, one horrifying step at a time, until she stood over me. Her black skirt billowed at her feet. I broke my gaze and lowered my head, looking at her shiny black boot. Fear coursed through me, rushing through my veins in a deafening thunder. Fear surpassed the agony of flesh torn open on my spine. I was silent.

She didn't bend over. She didn't speak kindly in my ear. Her voice was passionless, "You will learn. And I will teach you." Her boot scraped back, away from me. She flicked her wrist, and the process began again.

Flick by flick, she covered my body in lashes. By design, they tore open skin slowly, cutting through muscle, and nicking the bone. Every inch of me wanted to scream out and make it stop, but I didn't. Another lash sliced across my back. And then another. My hands moved frantically, trying to stop her, but there was no stopping her. Locoicia wanted me numb. And as long as I still felt my skin tearing apart she would not stop. Desperately, I tried to bite back pain, but it wasn't enough. It was never enough. There was no reprieve. There was no rest. Lash after lash fell on me. Eventually, I could no longer stand. My cheek pressed against the cold stone floor, lying where I fell. Locoicia's wrist flicked, again and again. She didn't stop until I didn't scream. She tormented me until I failed to flinch, until I was near dead by her feet.

My heart beat faintly in my ears. I felt nothing— not the pumping of my heart. Not the cool air slipping down my throat as I breathed. The rocks beneath my head were neither cold nor hard. The sensations that they produced did not affect me. Lying on my side, I stared at nothing. My eyes no longer throbbed. My throat no longer burned from the frantic screams that I bellowed. There was nothing. Numbness flooded every inch of me, cancelling out the pain that had been screaming in my mind for hours. The open flesh covering my body did not pain me. The blood seeping through my shirt was a fact, not a sensation. Strips of open flesh lined my back, and wrapped around my torso. Blood pooled underneath me, clinging to my waist and seeping through my shirt. My hair was tangled and bloody. There wasn't an inch of flesh that she didn't rip open. There wasn't any part of me that she didn't torment.

Locoicia stood over me with dead eyes. Her black boot was close to my head. My eyes stared, unblinking at her boot. My mouth hung open. She leaned down and whispered in my ear, "Kreturus would have captured you in seconds. He would have twisted your naive emotions into a tangle of truth and lies that you couldn't have navigated. Now you will feel nothing, and your ears will hear the truth." She paused. "You will thank me for this. One day, you will thank me for this."

CHAPTER FOURTEEN

My eyes flickered until I managed to pull the lashes apart. I was back in the warehouse. Alone. Every muscle in my body strained as I tried to move, and failed. Somewhere in the back of my mind, weariness unlike any I'd ever known called out to me. Sleep pulled at me, and I wanted nothing but to cave and allow the brief bit of rest that would restore me. I pushed my tangled hair out of my face, and slid my hands down my cheeks. Dried blood flaked off in my hands. My chest rose, as I took a shallow breath. I was weak, my muscles were frail. It was a fact, not a feeling. I knew what my body needed, but not yet. Not yet.

I pushed myself off the pallet I made on the floor, and leaned back on my arms. Halfway up. Another push and I sat upright. A swirling sensation in my head almost smashed my face into the floor, but I caught myself. I pressed my hands to my body wondering how badly I was hurt. My hands slid through holes that slashed my shirt. It looked like my shirt belonged to an eighty's rocker who didn't believe in safety-pins. The fabric barely hung on. I turned my head slowly, cracking my neck. Another breath, and this time it came easier. When I exhaled white vapor appeared in front of my mouth. I pursed my lips and blew it away. My skin was covered in goose-bumps. It was freezing—cold enough to snow. I'd have to move. Go somewhere warmer. Get dry.

Pushing myself off the floor, I slowly rose. My legs were stiff, and wobbled beneath my weight. I had to move. I had to get dry. Get warm. I effonated to the mall, and emerged gasping inside a stall in the women's bathroom. The stall door caught my body as I fell forward. My fingers slid down the cold metal. Pushing off the door, I righted myself. When I was ready, I unlatched the door and walked out of the stall. Three mirrors sat behind three sinks, across from three empty stalls. My hands reached out for the counter to support my weight in front of the center sink. Taking a deep breath, I straightened myself and looked in the mirror.

Dark brown patches crusted over pink welts on my arms and neck. One of the lashes had ripped up to my neck and onto my cheek. I pressed my fingers to the dried blood. I couldn't feel my own touch. The sensation registered, but it was only factual. My skin was dirty. My skin was cold.

I looked away, down at the sink and twisted the faucets. The warm water spilled out. I cupped it in my hands and washed away the signs of my torment. After I wiped off my face and arms, I staggered into the mall not caring what I looked like. That was the best I could do. People steered clear of me. My feet scraped the floor with an exhaustion that I couldn't fight off much longer. Looking for a store, any store, I picked one and walked inside. No one approached me. None of the sales people asked me if I needed help. They seemed grateful that I didn't want to try stuff on. Instead, I grabbed a pair of dark jeans, a blue pullover, and a black tee shirt and tossed them on the counter.

A perky blonde stifled a shocked expression when she looked up at me. I blinked once. She made no comment, just quickly tapped the keys on the cash register, and told me the price. She moved my purchases into a plastic shopping bag, while keeping her gaze off of my face as much as possible. I reached into my pocket for money I didn't have. I used my power. Paper bills lined my pockets. I pulled out the correct amount, and slapped it down. Without waiting for change, I grabbed my bag, and walked briskly out the door and into the main corridor of the mall.

The pain hit a moment later. My jaw locked and my body tensed, as the sensation of a hot knife punctured my stomach and slid up my throat. Muscle and flesh tore in a slow line. Heat rose from my navel to my throat. My pace did not falter. The expression on my face didn't contort with pain. My breath didn't ring out with cries. No tears streaked my cheeks. Numbness flooded me, until the pain subsided. I could still feel the pain price, but it was like a distant memory devoid of shape, form, or meaning. I knew it was happening to me, I could feel it, but it didn't matter.

Hastening my walk with the little strength that remained, I rounded the store corner, and walked back into the girl's bathroom. A fluorescent light flickered to life hesitantly. There was no one in the room. Walking quickly, I shoved my hand against the door of the center stall, and latched it. Turning, I leaned back. The dried blood on my back was pulled taught and then cracked. I'd never wanted a shower so much in my life. I just stood there. Exhausted. A moment passed. Then two. I took a deep breath and reached for the bottom of my shirt. But, before I could slip it over my head, I felt his presence. The sound of metal scraping came from the door, and then his footfalls echoed toward me.

I leaned my head against the metal stall door. Fatigue clawed at me. Soon there would be no option. Soon I wouldn't be able to maintain two feet on the floor. Locoicia sucked every drop of energy out of me. I could barely stand, never mind attempt to speak rationally enough to keep him away. I pressed my hands to my temples. I couldn't face him now. Blinking once, I moved my hands away from my face and looked at the tiled floor.

Black boots wet with winter snow appeared at the bottom of the stall door. "I need to see you." His words were simple and urgent. He stood with his feet apart, waiting.

I tried to mask the exhaustion in my voice. I stood, and stared at his boots. "Collin, no. Not now." After the words slipped out of my mouth, I leaned against the door of the stall. I stared at the chipped blue paint. The door was the only thing holding me up. I was so tired. Trying to hide these things from him required more strength than I had.

Without a word, without a warning, the door I was leaning against gave way. Collin pulled it off the hinges in one tug, and I fell forward. I never really had cat-like reflexes. I was about to collide with the floor when his other arm shot out and caught me. His hands brushed my shoulders, making me stand on my own two feet again, as he released me.

The room was swaying, tilting slowly to the right. My eyelids felt like sandbags. I smirked, "That was a little bit rash. Destruction of public property and all."

He gazed at me, but didn't smile. "Where have you been?" His eyes slid over my body, taking in my tangled hair and the white streaks that lined my skin. I hoped he didn't see the dried blood that caked under my clothes. "You look like hell."

I shrugged, "Same difference." A state of intoxicated weariness was drowning me. My muscles were protesting, threatening to stop working. But I held myself upright. After a moment, I relaxed when I didn't feel bombarded by sensations to press my body to Collin's. Whatever Lorren did to me seemed dormant right then. Although, Collin still looked beautiful. My eyes slid over his body, taking him in. His hair hung in soft waves, dark and wet from the snow. A black leather jacket hung opened from broad shoulders. The angle of his jaw was perfect, although it twitched as the little muscle flexed. A smile pulled the corners of my mouth, and I laughed. It was snowing.

Anger flashed in his eyes. "Don't play with me, Ivy." He placed the stall door on the floor and leaned it against the wall. When he turned back to me, his dark hair fell into his face. His eyes were on fire. Angry.

"You've been fighting someone. You're drained. And I saw you—I felt... " His hands stretched once, and then fisted tightly. He leaned in closer to me, causing my stomach to stir. His beautiful lips curved as he bit off the words in my face. "Who hurt you?"

I tried to sound nonchalant. I tried to brush off his concerns, "I'm fine, Collin. I really am." I stared at his jacket, avoiding his gaze. "I'm just tired. And I want to change." I held up the bag I'd been holding. For a second he stepped back, looked at my tattered clothes and then my shopping bag.

He stepped closer, and I stepped back. His eyes swept over me, making my breath catch in my throat. Collin's gaze rested on the line that extended from my shredded shirt and up my neck. His fingers touched the place and slid upward, tracing the line that marred my throat. When his fingertip touched my jaw, my head fell back nearly knocking me over. His hands gripped my arms tight. "Who's done this to you?"

I shook him off. Collin released his grip and my arms slid away. Angling away, I moved back. "No one," I whispered, finding myself unable to say her name. It wouldn't form in my mind either, no matter how hard I tried. I felt the vowels of her name tumble around in my mouth, but I couldn't purse my lips to say it. My voice wouldn't come. I realized that I couldn't tell him who did this, even if I wanted to.

Collin stepped closer. My eyes fell from his face to the hollow of his throat. His skin had a sheen from the snow. He took a breath, forcing his chest to rise. I watched as if I'd never seen him breathe before. My eyes suddenly lifted to his face. Collin's gaze slid over me like a careful caress. Swallowing, I stepped back again, trying to get away from him. Cold tiles pressed to my back as I hit the wall.

"Tell me." His eyes were cut into narrow slits, as he closed the space between us. His sweet intoxicating breath washed over my face. I breathed it in, and closed my eyes. Collin watched me do it. I was too tired. I couldn't help it. His body tensed and he stepped away from me. Cold air filled the space where he once stood. "What was that?"

I blinked slowly, feeling more and more relaxed by the second. My mind was weak from battling Locoicia. I needed sleep. I needed Collin. My lips pulled into a smile as I leaned against the cold wall. My voice was sweet, alluring. "What was what?" I slid my foot up the wall and pushed off, moving toward him.

The bond didn't choose sides, it simply revealed things if we weren't careful. Things we'd been hiding. In my state, I couldn't hide much of anything. Instead of asking, I felt Collin press into my mind. His presence was overwhelming. Anger clouded his thoughts as my recent memories flew by. He could see the pain, the practice, the demon blood being brought to life in my veins. His anger twisted into rage, and his eyes pooled bright crimson—like burning blood—as he pushed through my thoughts searching for the face of the one teaching me the things he forbade.

When he saw no face, he withdrew. I blinked slowly as if drunk, and inhaled his scent again. He leaned toward me, and bit into his lower lip. His nostrils flared as every muscle in his neck corded. "Who did this to you? Who's teaching you these things?"

"Careful, or you'll start your *Akayleah*." My eyes slid over the exposed skin on his neck, and then back to his face. He was perfect. Rage would only ruin him. "That would be a shame."

Collin's jaw flopped opened. He quickly snapped it shut. The intensity of his anger would have normally made me back away. But this time, I was content to have him near and I didn't care if he was yelling. And he was, but his voice washed over me, and I was too weary to hear his words. He demanded a name. His mind searched for a face—a face that didn't exist because I hadn't seen it. And the blood bargain kept me from revealing her name. It didn't matter how much he prodded me, he wouldn't learn who did this to me. He wouldn't learn that I volunteered for it, either.

Suddenly, my arms and legs felt like sacks of flour, pulling me hard. My knees bent and I started to slide down the wall. My head tilted to the side as I fought to keep my eyes open. Collin stopped ranting, and put his arms around my waist. His embrace felt so good, and his face was right next to mine. He was so warm and my skin was like ice. Without thinking, I brushed a soft kiss to his cheek. Collin tensed as my lips pressed against his skin. His breath caught in his throat, before he reached around with his other arm and lifted me. My head tilted back, and rested against his chest as my legs dangled over his arm. The grip on my back was perfect. I snuggled into his jacket. Collin watched me lying in his arms, as I started to drift off.

Collin's voice was soft, he pressed his face to mine and kissed the top of my head. He whispered, "If you only knew… "

CHAPTER FIFTEEN

Cracking my eyes open, I glanced around. A soft mattress lay beneath me, surrounded by four thick posters carved from dark wood. Glancing around the room, I saw no one, only bookcases of dark wood that stretched from the floor to the ceiling. The chair and table across from the bed were empty.

I was in Collin's room. And he was not here.

I slipped out of bed and padded to the door. Pressing my ear to the wood, I listened. Not a sound came through. When I turned, there was a mirror behind me. My tangled hair was crusted to my head. I pressed my hands to my face, and turned looking for the bathroom. Collin's room was enormous, filled with dark wood, dark carpets, and dark fabrics that all felt wonderful to touch. There was a pocket door at the back of the room. It slid open to reveal a gleaming ivory bathroom with dark fixtures. My bag was on the counter along with some towels. A glass container was next to the washcloth. I pressed down on the top and clear liquid came out. Raising it to my nose, I sniffed and closed my eyes. Body wash. And it smelled like Collin.

I closed the door and showered, dressing quickly. After brushing the knots out of my hair, I went to the massive window that stretched between the bookcases and pushed back the lush drapes. I wanted to feel the sunlight on my skin. I wanted some semblance of normalcy. Right then, my life felt perfect. When the drapes parted, I saw the lawn gleaming white with snow. It covered everything and left the world bright with its shimmering cold touch.

His hand on my shoulder made me jump. I squeaked and turned sharply. I clutched my heart. Collin stood behind me, but I didn't feel him approach. He held a cup of hot cocoa. I took it with thanks. My hands were freezing. I wondered if I'd ever be warm again.

Collin swallowed and looked past my shoulder and out the window. Tension lined his body, although I couldn't feel much of his thoughts. He seemed distant. Confused. I wondered if he was doing it on purpose.

I turned to him, lifting the cup of cocoa. "Thank you."

His eyes were lifeless, like melted wax from a blue crayon. They revealed nothing. "For what?"

I turned back to the window staring at the blanket of snow that covered the frozen earth. I raised the cup to my lips and took a sip. The lack of warmth in Collin's voice, the way he was acting—still defensive and angry—worried me. Why couldn't I sense the reason? The bond made it difficult to hide things, especially when it was so plainly painted across his face.

Looking down into my steaming cup, I answered, "For last night. I was exhausted... Thank you for taking me here." He nodded. I could feel the movement behind me. When I shifted my focus from the cup to his reflection in the glass, I grew more concerned. I studied his dark hair in the glass, wondering how he could be so hidden from me. How did he sneak up on me? That'd never happened before. My teeth grazed the side of my lip, as I worried. My gaze was locked on the window, too afraid to turn around.

But minutes passed, and Collin's expression didn't change. His eyes were dull and dark. The lines of his face creased, as he tried to maintain his composure. I should be able to hear his distress. I should have known. But I didn't. When I couldn't stand it anymore, when the silence was too deafening, I finally asked, "Why can't I *feel* you? Why are your thoughts hidden from me?" I turned toward him, looking up into his face. "Your mind, your feelings and thoughts… " my voice dropped to a concerned whisper. I searched his eyes looking for the answer. "I can't sense them."

His gaze shifted off the frozen window pane and down into my face. His hair tumbled forward, and he blinked once, slowly. Dark circles clung under his eyes. Weariness lined Collin's lips as they formed into a thin, straight line. He lifted his hand, and slowly moved his fingers toward the ends of my hair. I didn't flinch or pull away. The lack of sensation between us made it much easier for me to control my actions.

Lifting a curl, he affixed his gaze upon it, and then looked back at me, dropping the lock of hair. "I don't know." His jaw opened, as if he was going to say something else, but he snapped it shut and turned from me. My eyes slid over his back as he walked over to the bed, turned and sat down on the edge.

Stepping away from the window, I stared at him. He'd changed his clothes from last night. His hair was perfectly rumpled, his deep blue shirt clung to his body, revealing the subtle curves of his form. But something seemed wrong, in addition to the bond. Maybe it was because I couldn't sense him? His scent wasn't tempting me very much either—that sweet seductive fragrance that was enticing me only days ago, was so faint that I could barely catch his scent. I pressed my bare foot to the floor, growing more concerned with each step I took towards him. With each pace, I expected his scent to fill my mind with passionate thoughts. But it didn't. I took another step, and then another. Toward the bed. Towards Collin. But nothing happened.

My head tilted slightly. Damp hair hung in twisting curls that fell to my back. The black tank I bought covered me, but I still felt exposed under his gaze. Collin's eyes slid over me from where he sat on the edge of the bed. They rose from my bare feet, to my hips, slowly sliding over every curve until his eyes met mine. Collin leaned forward, resting his elbows on his knees, with his arms draped over his lap. Icy eyes, the color of midnight watched me. They were mysterious once again. His eyes revealed nothing. No thoughts. No desires.

One last step and I stopped in front of him. My gaze drifted across the room to a mirror. Inside its silvery walls I saw myself standing in front of him with damp hair and bare arms. My throat tightened as I watched Collin. My foot began to slide back, but he reached for my waist and pulled me to him. Shock shot through me, causing me to inhale sharply. He pressed his face to my waist, inhaling slowly. I rested my hands on his shoulders, and looked down at him. Collin's grip was pressed against me. I could feel every curve of each finger through my clothes. I could feel the strength of his hands as he held me.

But the bond was silent.

My desire was non-existent. If his hands were on me like this last year, my heart would have exploded in my chest. But now, I could feel his grip. I knew that Collin was there, and I could sense the pressure and weight of his hands on me, but it was like our connection was broken. The alluring nature of his touch was gone. Slowly, he turned his chin and looked up at me. I could see it in his eyes, in the hollowness that lined his face—he could sense it too.

The bond was broken.

I placed my hands on top of his, wanting to see if the skin on skin contact still worked. When the bond started, Collin could only hear me if we touched. Maybe it would still work. Looking into his eyes, I slid my palm over his hand. There was warmth, and it still brought comfort to feel his skin beneath mine, but there was no connection. I couldn't hear his thoughts. His mind didn't brush mine. There was only the touch of our fingers, not minds.

Collin pressed his eyes closed, pulled his hand out of my grip. His lips pressed together tightly, as if he were going to say something and changed his mind. I waited to hear him speak. I wanted to know if he was as shocked as I was. But the expression on his face kept my mouth shut. I didn't reach for him again, or ask him to tell me what he was thinking. The slant of his shoulders and the tension in his jaw said enough. He watched the floor, his eyes shifting back and forth, thinking. Silent. He no longer moved his gaze across my body. He wouldn't look at me.

Collin leaned forward and rose. His body pressed into mine because I didn't step back. I wouldn't allow him to leave without a word. The tight muscles in his chest moved against me as he stood. His gaze touched my face, but I couldn't hear his thoughts. I couldn't feel his emotions. My stomach stirred. My throat went dry as invisible threads of panic tightened around my neck.

Collin watched me with his lips parted slightly. His chest rose and fell with every breath he took, pressing against me. My fingers slid around his wrist. I raised his hand to my shoulder and placed it on the exposed skin on my neck. Collin watched me take his hands, and said nothing. Gazing into his beautiful face, I felt my breath catch in my throat. My jaw stiffened, as I tore my eyes away. Wrapping my fingers around his other hand, I put it on the back of my shirt. I moved his fingers down my back and to the bottom of my shirt. Collin's gaze remained locked on my face, as I placed his hand under the fabric and rested it directly on the warm skin at my waist. His arms were stiff. The embrace felt forced. Afraid. His gaze finally lifted from mine, when I lowered my lashes. I leaned into him and slipped my hands under his shirt, pressing my fingers to his back. I rested my hands on his waist, swallowing hard, and waiting for him to pull away. But he didn't. My touch gently moved across his taught muscles, feeling every dip and curve of his back.

Collin sucked in a small gasp of air when my hands pressed against him. And then neither of us moved. The sunlight streamed across the room, falling across Collin's face accentuating his perfection. His lashes lowered. They were dark against his smooth skin. His gaze fixated on my lips making me forget what I was doing. His lips parted as I watched him. Collin was so close. His scent filled my head making me forget what I was doing. I blinked once and turned my face from him. His eyes flew back to mine.

Suddenly, I remembered what I was doing, why I put his hands on me, and why I was touching him. *Collin?* I asked, brushing his mind with my thoughts. I breathed gently, too afraid to move. Too afraid to shatter the moment.

His eyes flickered with relief as he felt it. The emotion echoed back faintly in my mind. He smiled softly at me. *Ivy.* The way he said my name made me melt. The apprehension in his eyes faded when he felt the warmth of my skin. We could still hear each other. Closing his eyes, Collin pulled me to him, and pressed his face into the curve of my neck and breathed deeply.

Relief flooded me. I didn't realize how much he still meant to me until that moment. I was so mad at him. When Eric told me that Collin had fed me blood, more than once, I couldn't forgive him. I no longer trusted him. It didn't matter what he said or why. Feeding me his blood made it so I couldn't trust myself. I didn't know if I really loved him or if that was a side-effect of the demon blood. I didn't know if the bond was real either. And up until this point, I wished the bond would break. I didn't want the intrusion. I couldn't bear having Collin in my mind, not if he didn't love me.

But his hands on my body, the relief that erased the tension in his shoulders, and his inner sigh as I brushed across his mind—it made me realize something important. I believed him. Collin used his blood to heal me. If he had used his blood on me the way Eric did, I'd feel it. I'd feel it now more than ever. But I didn't. The emotions coming from Collin weren't lust-driven. They were deeper. He needed me in a way I didn't fully understand until that moment. There was passion, kindness, and a steadfast nature that seeped through his thoughts, as his cheek pressed against my neck.

And I needed him. I wanted him with me. I wanted his company. And it was more than his beautiful face, and more than the seduction of his voice. It was him. And everything about him. His determination. His compassion. His sense of humor and the way he saw the world. The way he made me laugh. The comfort he brought. It was him. I loved him. And I realized at that moment, that I always would.

The contact of his flesh against mine made something inside of me stir. My stomach twisted as Collin's thoughts pressed into me gently with a rush of affection I didn't expect. He pressed his lips against my neck. Every ounce of restraint broke as his lips touched me. Another kiss at the base of my neck made my knees buckle. Collin caught me in his arms, pressing my body tightly to his, as he lowered me onto the bed. He lifted his hands from under my back and kneeled, looking down at me. The sunlight surrounded him, making him look ethereal. His eyes were sparkling, full of life. He pressed one hand next to my head, and the other by my waist and lowered his body on top of mine, pressing into me.

My heart beat wildly in my chest and I finally felt warm. My arms reached around him, holding him tightly against me. When I released the embrace, my hands traveled along the curve of his back, feeling him against me. The weight of his body on top of mine made me feel sedate and giddy at the same time. Lightheadedness surged through me as every inch of my body felt like it was on fire. A soft smile slid across my lips, as I looked up at him.

I didn't want to release my grip on his waist. His skin felt so perfect. The moment was perfect. I wanted to press my lips to his, and feel the heat of his body against me—but I couldn't. That would never happen. That could never be. Lorren's warning pressed into the front of my mind, shifting my mood rapidly. I didn't want Collin to feel what Lorren had said to me. I didn't want him to know. I could feel the beat of Collin's heart, as his body pressed into me. His breath on my neck was jagged and warm.

Pressing my eyes closed, I savored the sensation before I slid my hands off his waist. They fell to my side, resisting the intense urge to run them through Collin's hair and pull his lips down on top of mine. It was getting so warm, and my mind was clouding. I couldn't tell him what Lorren did to me. I couldn't tell him that the kiss would steal my soul—and his—but we had to stop. Collin seemed to sense that the moment was over. He pressed a kiss to my cheek before he moved away. I sucked in a deep breath, as I felt him move across my body, every tight muscle in his chest sliding across me slowly until he was laying on the bed next to me. He tucked his hands behind his head and stared at the ceiling with a smile on his face.

Turning to him, I laughed, "Tease."

His gaze darted to the corner of his eyes, where he saw me, smirked, and let out a little laugh. Releasing one hand from behind his head, he took my hand in his and we both laid there for a moment, neither of us willing to move. I turned my head back toward him. His profile was regal perfection. The beauty of the slant of his nose and the angles of his cheeks were amplified by the golden sunlight that washed across his face. The entire bed was drenched in sunlight. It streamed in from the cold glass window panes, which were etched with vines of frost.

Collin turned and looked at me. His eyes had a flicker of bright blue within their depths again. I stared, unable to look away, afraid that the familiarity between us, the feeling of oneness, might slip away again.

Clearing my throat, I asked softly, "What happened to us?"

His gaze steeled. The bond was fleeting, like a snowflake pressing against the warmth of bare skin. In the past, laying there with him, and feeling his fingers intertwined with mine, would have been enough to open the floodgates of the bond. Everything would pour between us without a word. But, the faintness of the bond made my brow crease and the pit of my stomach feel like it was filled with glass.

Collin shrugged, looking away. "You. You did this." His fingers touched the thin white line that extended up my neck. The scar the Demon Princess inflicted would be gone in a few hours, but right then, there was still a welt. I stopped breathing as he traced the welt with his pointer, gently feeling my skin move beneath his hand. His bottom lip pushed into the top suddenly. I sucked in a breath as Collin sat up and snaked his hands around my back, lifting me off the bed. His palm pressed into me, as he pulled me up off the mattress. His eyes locked with mine as his fingers moved along my back, feeling the curve of my body and the many ridged scars that failed to heal. I could barely breathe, barely move. Collin's gaze tore into mine, searching through my mind, looking for the memory of who did this to me. But he didn't find it. There was no face. No memory.

I sat up, and his hands fell away. Collin shifted on the bed next to me, watching. I reached for the back of my shirt, and lifted it to expose my skin. I gazed into the mirror behind me. My eyes slid over too many ridges and welts to count. Many were still bright red.

Some were so thick that Collin's hand was not wide enough to cover them. My mouth hung open. My skin didn't heal. It should have been white like the scar at my neck that was fading, but it wasn't. None of them were. A maze of scars ran across my back covering every inch of me. I pressed my lips together, not comprehending their existence.

His voice shattered the silence, "This. This is what happened to us. This is what destroyed the bond." He gestured toward my back. His eyes pierced me and I wanted to weep, but there was no moisture in my eyes. He pressed his lips together, and shifted his eyes to my back. "Was it worth it? Did you want to be rid of me so badly?"

My eyes were wide, "No! It wasn't like that. I didn't know… "

Collin wouldn't let me look away from him. His eyes contained so much grief that I couldn't stand it. A moment passed before he spoke again. He reached for a loose curl and tucked it behind my ear. The back of his palm grazed my cheek as he withdrew his hand. "You could have heard me before. You would have heard how much you mean to me. There was no question," he shook his head, "But you didn't believe me, and you did this. I can't fathom it. I can't understand why you would do this. You're so close to losing every feeling you have. And it was all to push me away? It was to end your connection with me?"

"No, Collin. It wasn't like that. I didn't mean to… " Rubbing my hands over my face, I pushed back my hair and looked down at the bed sheets. Tiny creases formed folds in the smooth white cotton. "I had to. It wasn't optional." Swallowing hard, I turned my head upward and looked at the ornate ceiling. Dark stained wooden beams ran the length of the room.

"Everything is optional," he retorted. He didn't look at me while he spoke. "You did this. You chose this. I told you. " He could no longer speak. His throat released choked words, "I told you… How I felt. I told you the blood wouldn't harm you. I never wanted to push you away."

"I never wanted you to leave. Collin, I don't want to lose you."

"That's not what it looks like." He shook his head, refusing to look at me. He pushed his hair away from his face and turned away from me, hanging his leg over the side of the bed, ready to stand.

I reached for him, wrapping my fingers around his arm. He glanced down at my grip, and back into my face. My jaw hung open as I tried to find the right words and failed, "But it's the truth."

He laughed, leaning in toward my face. His lips brushing lightly against mine. My lower lip trembled as he spoke, "The truth. The truth is you make me crazy! The truth is you came here to torment me, sliding your hands over my body only to show me that you'd throw away the bond to be rid of me!"

I grabbed his hands, as his face searched the room, looking anywhere but at me. "No! You don't understand! It's not what happened. It wasn't like that!" When he didn't turn, I pressed my hands against his cheeks and turned his face toward me.

"Then explain it to me."

Blinking hard, I opened my mouth to speak, but couldn't find the words. Collin watched me. After several minutes of silence passed, he looked away. His muscles tensed as he was about to stand. The words I didn't want to say came tumbling out of my mouth. "I made a blood bargain."

He flung himself over me in a heartbeat, knocking me back on the bed. Oh God. His eyes! The expression on his face—it was as if I could see his heart shatter into a million tiny pieces and skitter across the floor. I sucked in a breath and tried to look away from his face, but he took my head in his hands and made me look up into his face. Blue eyes burned with rage as he looked down at me, as he bit back a mad scream. "How could you?"

His arms flexed once, hard, and he pushed himself off of me, and shot up. When his feet hit the floor, the muscles in his arms and chest were ripped into tight cords, bulging through his shirt. His hands pressed to his mouth, as he stared at nothing. Horrified. His open hand curled into a fist. He turned, and crossed the room with a speed that made me gasp. Collin drew back his shoulder and released a punch that connected with the wooden bookcase, splintering the ornately carved wood. He rounded on me as shards of wood flew through the air. His shoulders, his muscles, his neck were all so strained that I couldn't look away. My heart raced in my chest, but no fear slid into my stomach. I didn't feel the need to run. Collin effonated to the bed, and jumped next to me, catching my shoulders as his weight threw me in the air and throwing me down on the bed. His hands slammed down on either side of my head. Collin held me still with his chest, locking me in place with his arms. "Why? Why? Why would you do such a thing?" he screamed in my face.

For a moment there was nothing but the sound of my breath as he waited for a response. It was a response I couldn't give. I did it because I had to. I did it because I had no choice. Finally words came to me, "I did it because you can't protect me from him forever." Collin's jaw twitched as it locked tight. My heart roared in my ears. It felt like I was yelling, but my voice came out in a whisper. "There is no way out of the prophecy, Collin. You know that. This won't end, not until I end it." He shot away from me, like I was poison. Jumping upright, I crawled off the bed on my knees. His back was to me. Every muscle in his body looked as if it could explode. I didn't touch him. "Collin, I didn't want it to affect us. I didn't know… "

He rounded on me. Within seconds he was in my face. "But I did. I told you the price was too high. I told you nothing was free. Not when demons are involved. And now you are bound to this demon until he's done with you… if he doesn't kill you first! And how are you going to live with this?" He thrust a finger forward, pressing it against the place where the venom laid in my chest.

I shook my head, swatting his finger away, trying to keep him from seeing what Locoicia did. "Collin, it's not like that. You don't understand." My arms reached behind me, as I tried to move away from him, crawling backwards across the bed.

Collin leaned down into my face, roaring. Angry. Afraid. "No! You don't understand! They don't play by the rules. They aren't fair. Anything, and everything they say is covered in lies! Damn it, Ivy!" His hands shot to his hair, where he pulled. He hesitated, his arms shaking. When he turned back to me, Collin's eyes were wild, burning like the blue flame at the center of a massive fire. Collin reached for me. I didn't realize what he was doing until it was too late. His fingers grabbed my neckline and pulled hard. The fabric tore like a tissue in his hand. The piece of dark cloth fell away. Shocked, I stood there with my mouth hanging open. My instincts were too slow. My hands hesitated. Before my arms shot up to cover me, his eyes saw it. Smooth skin. No trace of the venom that was killing me.

His lips parted as he looked into my face, as his eyes narrowed to untrusting slits. I cracked my jaw to speak, but he reached for me. His hand shot out, pulling my arms away from my chest. Then his thumb slid along the top of my bra, making my heart leap into my throat. He stared at the patch of soft, white flesh. There was no dark line marring my breast. The sapphire serum appeared to be gone. There was nothing but smooth skin. Twisting out of his reach, I grabbed the remnants of my shirt and clutched them to my chest.

I wanted him to understand, but he didn't. He couldn't. He sucked in a sharp breath and dropped his hand. "He healed you." His words were scarily calm. His eyes were suddenly sucked free of anger. Looking into my face, he asked, "What was the price?" My lips parted, but I couldn't speak. I leaned away from him. "What was the price!" Turning abruptly, he snapped off one of the posters and hurled it across the room. The massive piece of carved wood slammed into the bookcase, tearing away a chunk of wood as it bounced away, and shattered the mirror. Shards of glass flew through the room, sprinkling across the floor like a can of spilled glitter.

"Collin, stop!" I screamed. He turned slowly toward me. His back was curved, ready to fight. Crimson pooled in his blue eyes making them burn like hot coals. Gasping, I backed away from him. Nothing I said would reach him now. Not like this. I tried to slide past him, but he caught my arm. His fingers pressed hard into my flesh. I moved to twist out of his grasp. There was something in his eyes I hadn't seen in a very long time.

Lust. The desire for a demon kiss. His eyes fixated on me. Their intensity made me feel entirely naked. It was as if I'd been stripped of everything as I stood before him. My breath caught in my throat.

Nodding slowly, talking softly I pressed my fingers on top of his hand—the hand that held my arm. "It's all right. It's all right, my love." I slowly peeled away his fingers as I felt his grip loosen. "You're starving… " I asked looking into his eyes as I peeled away another finger. "Aren't you? It'll be all right, Collin. Just breathe. Breathe and I'll help you." I peeled away the last finger. An inky bruise was blossoming in four narrow patches where he'd held me. I ignored it. It would fade. Collin fought every instinct he had. His eyes remained locked on mine. I couldn't look away. When I'd freed my arm,

I placed my hands on his face and stroked his cheeks, slowly speaking softly to him until the tension that made his body shake ebbed.

CHAPTER SIXTEEN

As I watched him fight for control of himself, I could see it in his eyes. Collin's eyes swirled with deep red flames, burning bright, around the outer iris. The center of his pupil was a tiny black dot. And every shade of flame and fire burned in between. It moved as if liquid within his eyes. Slowly, slowly the reds faded to oranges, and then swirls of blue appeared. They were nearly stripped of color initially, but as I rested my palms on his cheeks, I saw his eyes return to the color of the sea after a storm.

Leaning toward him, my hands were still on his cheeks. He blinked, and looked down, breaking the gentle hold I had on his face. "I'm sorry." He rose and walked away from me. His arms were folded over his chest. He stared at the floor, seeing nothing. "I denied myself too long. It made me... weak."

I remained where I was, sitting on the floor looking up at him. "You don't have to do everything on your own." My words drifted through the air like a dandelion caught in the wind. He turned toward me slowly with a pained expression on his face. "My fate is set in stone... " I smiled sadly, "It's set. I can't change it." I rose and walked over to him. I stopped in front of him, looking up to catch his gaze. "You can't change it. You can't protect me from this. I have to do it myself. And I need you to let me."

He glanced down at me. His arms were still folded tightly, pressing into his chest. "You and I... " he stumbled over his words. The tense posture he held melted and his arms fell to his sides. Turning his head away from me, he ran his hands through his hair. "You and I... " his mouth hung open. It was as if he wanted to say something but couldn't. "Our fates... our destinies are intertwined, Ivy. If you accept one part of the prophecy, then you have to accept all of it." His fingers reached for the hair on my shoulder. He pressed the long curl between his fingers, and looked up at me. "Is that what you want?"

Shaking my head, the brown curl fell away. I stepped toward him, "What are you talking about?"

His lips parted, as his eyes shot to the floor. A dim smile pulled at the corner of his mouth. "I die. The prophecy says I die. You and I cannot coexist if the prophecy is fulfilled." He shook his head as if it could undo the words.

My gaze fell to the floor as my jaw dropped open. "I thought that had already come to pass?" Collin's eyebrow arched as he looked at my face. "On Long Island, the night of the Valefar attack… " I sighed shaking my head… suddenly shaking all over, "Didn't it? We changed it, didn't we?" My eyebrows rose as I spoke, saying words that I knew weren't true. My fingers were at my mouth, pressing on my lips as I thought.

The look on his face said we didn't change a thing. The look on his face said I didn't realize things yet. He shook his head. A wan smile made him look more sad than happy. "Nothing's changed. If you accept the prophecy is real, you accept all of it. You will defeat Kreturus, and become the Demon Queen. The world will end at your hands. The Martis will be destroyed. The Valefar will be annihilated. You will cause the gates of Hell to be flung open and the innocent to perish… " His eyes searched my face as he spoke. He looked away, his voice dropping to a whisper, "And I will die. It's my fate, as this is yours."

Something was choking me. I couldn't breathe. My throat was so tight that air would not slide down it and into my lungs. What did Locoicia do to me? My body still responded to his words, but I couldn't feel the warnings my mind shot out. Fear would have told me what was going to happen. The sensation of dread pooling in my stomach would have prompted me to speak. But I didn't. Instead, I stared at Collin, unable move.

His words were words I'd heard before, but never really accepted. Collin told me that the prophecy said he would die by my hand. It was as clear as me being the one to cause the floodgates of Hell to burst open. But that part, Collin's death, the Martis weren't concerned about. I didn't hear it over and over again. I pushed the thought to the back of mind, hoping that it was no longer true. Of the paintings I'd seen in the Lorren, the prophecies of death and destruction—not one showed me killing the boy who stood in front of me. But I knew that part of the prophecy, and I'd been fighting it. Denying it. I denied it until I accepted Locoicia's help. Until I made the bargain.

My gaze rushed to Collin. He stood motionless, waiting for me. Waiting for me to realize what he already knew. The prophecy destroyed everything, and everyone.

Even him.

There was no justice. There was no happy ending. These things would come to pass, and I was the one who caused them. I gaped, my jaw hanging open, trying to speak—trying to breathe.

Collin lifted his hands and rested them on my cheeks. His head tilted to the side. Dark brown hair slid into his eyes, eyes that sparkled like brilliant blue gemstones. Eyes that would cease to exist because of me. "I can't accept it. I can't accept the prophecy. It's not my fate. I can't let it be. I'll fight it 'til I die." He shook his head. There was a sadness deep within that laced his voice. "But, it sounds like you already have accepted your fate. In which case, we are enemies. Ivy… " he blinked once before he pulled his grip away, before he pulled himself out of my life. "This is the en… "

I cut off his words, his horrible words, and snatched his hand, shaking my head—shaking all over. "No. No, you can't be serious. This doesn't end this way. It doesn't!"

He pulled away from me again, and looked down. "We both know how it ends, but I can't accept it. I have to fight." He reached for a loose curl, twisting it in his fingers as he spoke, "I always thought that we'd find a way, you know. I thought you and I could change things." He dropped the curl and stepped back. "But, there's nothing we can do. And I can't sit around and wait for my death. I have to leave. I have to fight it—I have to." His foot slid away, another step that felt like a mile. "And I… I am the reason why it began in the first place." His gaze flicked to mine, and then broke again. "There are words I can't say, just as there are words you can't say. Blood bargains. Names. Things I'm sworn to do. Things I wish," he pressed his eyes closed and breathed.

When he looked back up at me again, his gaze was distant. Cold. "Beware the one you made your blood bargain with. Break it if there is any possibility. It is the only way you'll win. The demons twist words, they twist meanings… " he swallowed hard, staring at me like he'd never see me again. He pressed his lips together and spoke, "I can't say more than that. Don't default on your end of the bargain, but try to break it. Please." Heat began to build around him. He was going to effonate. I'd never see him again.

My eyes were wide. Panic choked my throat, but I couldn't feel it. Numbness tingled, covering my entire body. "Collin. You can't leave. We can't end things like this." The heat stopped. My heart stopped, jerking in my chest. My jaw hung open. My lips were silent, not speaking things that were locked in my heart—things he'd never hear.

Collin looked down, away from me. There was something in his face, a desperation that made him say the words, "Then join Kreturus and end this." Shock kicked me in the stomach as the words tumbled out. I lurched back away from him as my mouth hung open. He half smiled, "There is no other way to for this to stop. There are two choices; you fight him to the death… Or you join him." The corners of Collin's lips twitched as they pulled into a smile so soft and fragile. The shock of his words were still choking me like fingers around my neck. I didn't speak. Collin's gaze swept over me. "I knew you wouldn't join him," his voice was soft, accepting the unacceptable. "Everyone knows you won't join him, but that's the only scenario in which you and I are both still breathing in the end."

Shaking my head, I said, "It's not fair. It's not." I stared up at him, knowing that we'd never be alone again. We'd never have another moment. My eyelids pressed shut as I felt moisture build behind them. Collin's fingers stroked my cheek. I gazed up at him.

He dropped his hand and heat surrounded him again. He'd be gone in an instant. "Break the bargain. Pray for a mistake." His body was absorbed and the intense heat that surrounded him was quashed as quickly as it formed.

I stood alone in Collin's bedroom. I was surrounded by shattered, splintered, cracked, broken... things.

I was one of those things.

The bond was broken. And I was the one who broke it. It was fading. Dying. The bond was a distant echo of what had once been a powerful connection.

Collin was gone. He would die if I didn't join Kreturus. I couldn't. I wouldn't. Everyone knew.

Collin would die. Collin will die... because of me. There wasn't enough air.

CHAPTER SEVENTEEN

Eric. I needed Eric. He'd know what to do. But he was crazy. I kicked a snow drift as I walked through its center outside of Collin's home. The dry snow flew through the air and back into my face. It stung like little needles as it clung to my skin and melted on contact. The Valefar were gone. The Martis were gone. No one was here. I was alone. I wiped my face with a gloved hand. I'd borrowed some of Collin's winter clothes, since I had none. The leather coat smelled like him. My fingers slid into his gloves and made me remember his hands on my body. I suppressed the memory.

It was pointless.

And to make matters worse, I actually thought about giving myself to Kreturus. The lack of his presence concerned me, but just because I didn't see him, didn't mean he wasn't nearby. Maybe he made Collin say those words. Pressing my eyes closed, I walked onward through the snow, to nowhere. I could effonate, but I needed to feel something. I let the cold bite into the flesh on my face, as snowflakes and wind whipped through my hair. My curls were wet as they clung half frozen to my shoulders.

Eric. Eric knew where the Satan's Stone was. That rock could be the answer to everything. It could undo everything. It could heal me, free Collin, and stop the war that was about to begin. The gates of Hell could not and would not open. Not if I could stop it. The stone could stop it. The stone had stopped it before.

Maybe Collin was right. Maybe I hadn't accepted my fate. I didn't have time to consider it. I had to find that stone. I had to find Eric. It surprised me that Eric made no effort to find me after our last meeting. I kicked more snow into the air. Speckles of white blinded me for a moment as I walked through the cloud of snow. The sting on my skin felt good.

Since I'd been learning from Ilecica, my ability to feel sensations had been hindered. Hindered is the wrong word. My ability to feel was out of whack. I felt some things, but not others. It made me wonder if I could feel my arm if I set it on fire. I didn't understand how I could feel good as Collin's hands slid over my skin, but not feel the right emotions when he left. The entire time he spoke, it felt like someone was strangling me. If I'd felt something –anything—besides invisible fingers squeezing the air out of my lungs, maybe I could have changed things. Maybe I could have convinced Collin that we weren't enemies. But I didn't. And now he was gone.

I kicked another pile of snow and walked through it. Eric. I had to find Eric. He could find Satan's Stone. He had the book. My fingers tensed, as I thought about it. I needed that rock. That stone was my salvation. That stone had fabled power that was stronger than any of us. I had to get my hands on it, but Eric had the book—the useless book that no one could read. The book that connected things Eric had once known about Satan's Stone. Things he forgot because of me. It didn't matter. He had the book. That was enough. We'd figure out how to read it, and I'd kill him if I had to. Screw Lorren and his ward.

My eyes scanned the winter white blanket of ground in front of me. I walked. My feet crunched over snow and ice and frozen ground. Barren trees stuck up out of the snow like bony hands reaching for the warmth of the sun. A smile slowly slid across my frozen face. I knew where he'd be. Without another thought, I effonated to the place.

CHAPTER EIGHTEEN

Eerie quietness surrounded me as I shrouded myself with shadows, calling them to me like ink seeping into a quill. They moved towards me quickly. Quietly. Their corpse-like fingers stroked my throat and stomach as they entered me, but I no longer felt the pain. The sound of snow filled my ears as it fell from the heavens and softly touched the earth. It was utterly quiet.

The brown building stood in stark contrast to the pure white that covered its roof like a woolen blanket. The building itself was dark. Not a single light was blazing within the windows of St. Bart's. I stood at the side entrance on the inside of a seldom used door, and moved through the shadowed hallways. Cobwebs clung to the corners of the walls, filling nooks with silvery threads. A thick layer of dust carpeted the dark wood floors making it look as if it snowed inside. There wasn't a single footprint to be found. The building was deserted. No one had been here since Al left. The nuns had left. The church was gone.

This was no longer holy ground.

Eric was here. I was sure of it. My feet slid down the darkened halls puncturing the perfect dust, leaving long trails on the floor behind me. Turning, I saw the entrance into the nave. Moving ever so slowly, I slid one foot at a time—one breath at a time—until I was near the back rows of benches. Sunlight poured in through an overhead window making small beams of light pour down from the ceiling. Within the beams dust danced as it fell softly to the floor. Sliding past pews, I remained in the shadows, moving through the darkness still half frozen from being soaked by the snow.

A lone figure sat with his back to me at the front of the church. He was arrogantly sitting on the altar with his legs hung over the sides. His hands gripped the wooden table as he looked up to the colored glass high above. The bright winter sun shone through the window casting a kaleidoscope of color on the dark carpet. The patchwork of color also touched Eric's arms and head. He held out his fingers, twisting his wrist, examining the light as if he were holding a piece of sunshine in his palm.

I slid my feet closer and closer. There wasn't a sound. Not a single noise that let him know I was so close. So very close. My comb was already drawn. The tines were extended. I barely breathed as I neared his back. The wood altar under him was in the way, but the element of surprise was too great to throw away. I made my decision. Sliding up behind him, I got so close that if I breathed, he'd feel me. As Eric continued to contemplate the colored glass, I moved my head so that my mouth was next to his right ear.

And I breathed his name as I exhaled softly, "Eric."

His spine straightened, as his back lost its relaxed curve. He tried to jump off the altar to his feet, but my arms snaked around his neck faster than he could blink. Yanking him backwards with one swift pull, he fell off the slab of wood, and lay in the center aisle with his back to the floor. Shocked golden eyes were wide as the air was knocked out of his lungs. Eric gasped for air, momentarily stunned. Before he could move, I straddled his chest, placing one knee on each side of him. The silvery tines of my weapon touched his throat. His skin hissed as he tried to press himself into the floor. He couldn't try to throw me off without pressing the silver deeper into his throat. Eric's body tensed and became perfectly still beneath me.

"Miss me?" A wicked smile pulled at the corners of my mouth as I leaned forward, lifting the tines slightly so they no longer touched his skin. The smell of burnt flesh dissipated. If Eric took a deep breath, the tines would resume full contact. Every single one.

Rage shook his body, as muscles rippled and contorted, but somehow he managed to keep himself perfectly still. He snarled at me, "What do you want?" That wasn't the question I expected Eric to ask.

My bottom lip turned down, "No, you're supposed to say, 'How would you like to die?' or something more Eric-ish." I pressed the tines to his skin again. His lips pressed together so tightly that they disappeared into his mouth for a moment. I pulled back the tiniest amount and released him from the pain.

I wondered if I would feel pain like that anymore.

Eric tried to move his arms, but I was faster and stronger, which delighted me. I pressed my knees closer to his sides, pinning him in place, and making it so he couldn't expand his rib cage to breathe. Eric's golden eyes rimmed with fire. Something in his temple ripped as if it were ready to pop. "Kill me or get off of me, Ivy."

"As you wish," I smiled at him, rose, and before I took the tines away from his throat, I saw a smug smile form on his lips. It pissed me off. With a swift movement, I pressed the tines into his throat. They slowly slid into his flesh as I kneeled on his chest forcing my knees into his gut. I'd fall off in half a second, but he'd be dead by then… at least he thought he would.

A scream ripped from his lips as Eric expected the tines to press all the way into his neck, one by one. But they held. The tines remained above the muscle, just under the skin, as if he were made of stone. It didn't matter how hard I leaned, the blades would sink no further. I stared down at Eric. Dark hair cascaded over my shoulders. When he saw my face, when it registered that I didn't kill him, I pulled back my blades and jumped up. His hands flew to his throat. Eric's eyes were burning like spun gold set on fire. Rage pumped his muscles into bulges and flared his nostrils. He shot up and threw himself at me.

But I remained perfectly still with a soft smile on my face. My heart pounded against my ribs, but I didn't move. I didn't flinch. I didn't blink. Eric abruptly stopped whatever assault he had planned. My lack of motion unnerved him. Maybe it wasn't such a bad thing to feel no fear? I stood there with a smirk on my face watching him. Eric looked as if he didn't know what would happen next. His hands dropped to his sides, but his shoulders remained tense and ready to pounce. We stared at each other, circling slowly, our eyes never parting as one foot stepped over the other slowly turning. The smile remained affixed to my face as we turned. It was like a dance, two people moving with thought and caution, carefully placing each foot, and fighting to be the lead.

After several turns, I asked, "Are we just going to dance around all day?" I smiled widely, crouching my body forward, beckoning him to come to me with my hands. "Come get me."

Eric's gaze never left my face. His hands were outstretched at his sides. The veins in his arms circled beneath his skin corded like thick ropes. His foot turned and slid, mirroring my movements, but making no effort to attack. His lips rippled as he replied, "Finish this. Take what you came for, or leave. I have no time for your games."

I laughed. I couldn't help it. My back straightened and the sound escaped my belly before I realized why it happened. Eric paused, no longer moving his feet, but he did not straighten his spine. He remained bent toward me, ready to attack. "Why were you playing with the light? It was like watching a cat with a sunbeam. If you had a tail, it would've been flicking back and forth." I folded my arms over my chest. We had stopped circling.

Eric's spine slowly straightened, but his hands remained flexed at his sides. "What do you want?" His words were sharp. His voice held an uncertainty that I was waiting to hear.

Shadows spilled across his face as he straightened, making it look like he was wearing a mask. Sunlight poured onto the top of his head. His hair looked like golden silk in the sun. Wild. Unkempt pieces of gold as lustrous as his burning eyes. Eyes that slid over my body and back to my face.

"I have something you'll want to know." A smile tugged my lips, as I leaned back against a pew, putting more distance between us. Shafts of sunlight pierced the darkness between us. "There's a ward on you. You can't die."

Eric's mouth opened, but he only managed to swallow air. The things that flashed across his face ranged from disbelief, to anger. When he finally spoke he said, "That's what I felt, before? That's what I felt last time?" The ring of fire around his golden irises extinguished as he thought. "It felt like a piece of lead smashed down on top of me." He spoke as if speaking to no one, his gaze not focused on anything. Silence filled the room for three heartbeats before his neck snapped up and he glared at me, "And then you were gone." He took a step back, leaning his back against the altar. All the tension still lined his body. He didn't trust me.

I nodded as I tilted my head, and pressed my arms tighter into my chest. My wet hair clung to my back. I was freezing, but no one could tell. No one would see the pain of the chill deep in my bones. No one would see me shiver or shake ever again. "Mmmm. Some things need to be demonstrated to be learned."

His gaze locked onto mine and didn't waiver. His lips were thin. His jaw was locked. He cracked it to ask, "Who placed the ward on me? Who wants me alive?" The tension in his body increased and the curve of his spine straightened. His eyes were narrowed to thin slits.

Pushing myself off the pew, I paced slowly and looked over my shoulder at him. "Me," I lied. The look of shock on Eric's face made me smile. He believed me. Good. "You needed to realize that you can't control me," my voice deepened and was no louder than a whisper, "with your blood. You cannot hurt me with your lies. If I chose to, I could kill you with my bare hands. I placed the ward. I can remove it. I'm the one who saved you."

His brow pinched together as his fists balled, "You didn't save me, you destroyed me," he hissed. He shot across the room, stopping right before his nose pressed into my forehead. He glared down at me. Every hideous emotion was painted across his face. His eyes burned with rage that was focused singularly on me. He extracted a brimstone blade from his pocket. The movement was quick, faster than I could blink. The tip of the blade touched the top of his forefinger. A ribbon of scarlet snaked down his tapered finger, pooling in his palm. A wicked smile spread across his lips as he held out his bloodied hand in front of me.

Unblinking, I gazed at him. A deep hatred flared within me, white hot. Eric's blood made my limbs feel alive, and the pit of my stomach swirled as if it were filled with butterflies. The drop of red made my mouth burn. It burnt for him, for his blood in all its scarlet beauty that dripped down his fingers and slid down his wrist. All this warred within me, but I did not move. I did not blink. I could still feel, but the sensations were distant, as if they were someone else's thoughts hovering at the back of my mind.

Without a word, I reached out for Eric's hand. His eyes were wide as I took his bloody finger and softly pressed it to my lips. The warm slick substance pooled on my lower lip and slid down my chin. Opening my mouth slowly, I flicked out my tongue and slid it over Eric's finger tasting his blood. Elation washed over his face. Deep within me, something was screaming as if it was being buried alive. It called out to me, to stop, to feel, to do anything but this… But I didn't stop.

As my tongue flicked the tip of his finger, I swallowed. Then, I lowered his bloody hand and released it. I could still feel the weight of his arm in my grip. Never blinking, never speaking, I gazed into his amber eyes and slid my tongue over my lips—licking away his blood with the slide of my tongue. Eric's mouth slid into a slow smile, as he began to speak, but my hand darted up and I pressed a single finger over his lips.

Leaning in close, so close I nearly kissed the finger that separated us, I whispered, "You no longer own me."

Eric's chest constricted as if he'd plunged headfirst into an icy river. The fear in his eyes said he was drowning in slow motion. His jaw hung open as he stared at me. The only words he uttered was, "How?"

I laughed. My voice was deep, deeper than usual. More sensual. More confident. I felt my power. I felt it without rage, and I grabbed on. Leaning into his face, I pressed my nose to his. Our eyes locked. Fear flashed behind his orbs of gold. "Does it matter? Does it truly matter how I can resist you?" Pulling away slowly I felt the weight of my words slam down on his shoulders. "You're mine. Eric. I made you. I claim you. I deny you, and I control you. Your fate is in my hands. So choose. Death or... me." My eyes didn't waiver, my words didn't falter as my tongue wrapped around the lie. I did not make his ward. I cannot kill him, but he didn't know.

His eyes said they believed me. His gaze said he feared me.

Eric cast his gaze downward. Questions played across his face at a mile a minute. His hands balled into fists at his sides. He finally looked up and said, "I loathe you with every fiber of my being. I will not be satisfied to see your dead body beneath my feet." He moved slowly toward me, menace in his voice and violence in his stance. "It is not enough to feel your heart wither and die in my hands. You have taken from me more than you'll ever know, and I will take it back in any way I can." His fingers flexed at his sides. Eric's eyes were liquid gold, molten, burning and deadly. He swallowed hard. "What do you want from me?"

My heart felt like it was going to explode. My body still reacted to him, to his blood. I just learned to mask the desires and fears. They no longer danced across my face. I could no longer feel the fear within my racing heart. My words slid out with ease, "I want you to help me find the Satan's Stone, but first, I need you to answer something." He let out a short breath, enraged. "Why did you kill Al?"

CHAPTER NINETEEN

His lips smashed together and he turned away from me. I grabbed his shoulder and spun him back around. I thought he would snap off my head with his teeth. His jaw was so tense that he could have. "Answer me," I commanded.

His eyes were slits. His entire body shook as if it were ready to strangle me, but invisible wires held him in place preventing him from doing so. "I needed the book. Something happened, and I snapped. I did anything it took to get it. I said things to you and Collin. I taunted the nun as if I didn't know her, but when… when she fell, it came flooding back. Everything was there." He tore his shoulder out of my hand. "I don't know what happened. I didn't mean to kill her. She… " He looked at me from under his brow and turned away.

My feet remained still. The only indication that time was passing was the slow methodic breathing of my body. I stared at his back, mostly talking to myself. I don't know why I said it. I wasn't entirely certain that I believed him, but Lorren's observations made sense. I spoke to his turned back. "Kreturus was there. He was slowly separating me from everyone. Ties were broken. He put seeds of doubt in my mind… " I shook my head. Eric turned, looking over his shoulder. "If I'd done as I originally planned, you'd be dead. Shannon would be dead. And Al is gone. And Collin," I shook my head. "I'd be alone—like he wanted. I think it's what Kreturus set out to do."

Eric turned to me, suddenly much more interested. His words were sharp. He demanded, "And what about Collin? Where is he?"

My mouth hung open. Soft breaths spilled over my lips, but I couldn't bring myself to say it. I stared at Eric with my arms folded over my chest, pressing them down tightly to try and kill any remnants of the lingering sensations I had about Collin. Numbness flooded me. And I welcomed it. My gaze returned to Eric's, "And nothing. There is no one. Nothing. Kreturus successfully isolated me. It was his plan.

Without help, I'd be weak. I'd need him to survive. He used you. He used you to get at me."

Eric's eyes flicked to the side, and returned to my face. "It was still my hand. And it is still my mind that harbors the memories." He swallowed hard, casting his gaze away from me. Away from judgment. Away from the shame that pressed on his shoulders.

His dark shirt was rumpled as if he slept in it. But Eric didn't sleep. His arms were folded over his chest as he gazed across the room. Something had been bothering me about him, something that I didn't want to ask. But I had to know. "Why do you remember anything? You said things that night. Things you couldn't possibly know." I stepped toward him. Eric didn't move. I took another step, but Eric kept his gaze cast toward the floor. His lips were pressed tightly. I stopped next to him, next to his side, next to his ear. My voice wasn't commanding. It was soft, as if asking a child to reveal a great secret, "Will you tell me?"

He turned toward me. My breath caught in my throat. Remorse was strewn across his face. It hung there plain and thick, pulling him down toward the pits of Hell where he belonged. My jaw opened, but I was speechless.

"It's you," he said. "It's something to do with you. I can feel remorse. I can feel… " he sucked in air as if there weren't enough, and looked at me. "Shit, Ivy. You made Valefar that can feel. What was the one thing I told you? The one thing all Valefar wanted?"

"Power."

He nodded, "And that they'll do anything to get it because they don't feel a damn thing. But me," he glared at my face with hidden pain seeping through his eyes, "I feel everything. I feel it because of you. Because I remember." He shook his head, turning away from me and pressed his fingers to his temples. "I remember, because of the kiss."

I shook my head, not understanding, "What kiss? The Demon Kiss in the Lorren? What are you talking about?"

He turned to me, a lazy smile on his face. "Your kiss. I asked you to kiss me after I was a Valefar. Remember?" His golden eyes searched my face. My stomach flipped. "You did. And I stole from you when you did it. I took back some of the pieces of my life. My essence still lingered in you. It still does." He looked away, the smile fading. "You hold the key. You hold my memories."

"No," I replied moving closer to him. My face scrunched together, "That's not possible. You can't steal back your memories. They died with you. Otherwise you'd remember. You'd know things… " I paused with my mouth hanging open. He'd know where the Satan's Stone was. He'd remember taking his pen to that book of his and making the markings that no one could read. My eyes shifted, examining his face.

Eric shrugged, turning from me. "Say what you want, but it's what happened. Your demon kiss isn't the same as other Valefar. Maybe it's because you're not a Valefar. I don't know." He ran his fingers through his hair, and looked over his shoulder at me. "I just know that with each kiss, I was able to steal back bits and pieces of things I no longer knew. Things from my previous life. Things I'm not supposed to remember." He pushed his hair out of his face. It fell in no particular direction, each strand of hair doing its own thing.

I stared at him. He hated me with such raw intensity that I could sense it wafting off of him. A kiss from him could destroy me. He could steal the rest of my soul. It made me wonder how badly he wanted his memories back. Was it enough to keep me alive? My eyes slid over his hard body, still rigid, still tense. He didn't trust me either.

"What do you remember?" I asked. He cast a glare at me that would have made me gasp if I could feel, but I couldn't. So I glared back. He spoke. And once he started, words poured out of his mouth in an unending wave. He didn't remember many things, but he had some memories of things long ago—memories that I didn't own. Memories that weren't mine. They were a jumble of scenes, places, and people that made no sense to him. He spoke for nearly an hour when the words stopped. He tilted his head, and stared at me with such longing that my throat tightened in response. Foolishness comes in spurts that appear to be bravery. I had to know why my kiss was different. I had to know if the old Eric existed in some way inside of me. If he did… I had to know.

I moved in front of him, standing within his reach. Looking up into his face, I said, "Kiss me." Confidence rang in my voice. "Take a memory."

Eric hesitated. His eyes bore into me, tearing apart each inch of me with razor sharp hatred. His gaze narrowed as he walked toward me. His head tilted down, his eyes hardened and ruthless. The ring of fire in his eyes ignited around each pool of gold as he moved. He stopped in front of me. My heart was pounding in my chest. I could hear it, but the feelings were distant—like a memory. The lack of fear made me reckless. It made me feel alive. His hand shot behind my head, and his fingers snaked around the back of my neck, pulling me to him. The muscles under his shirt bulged. Each one was hard and smooth. I could sense his stomach, his chest, and his arms through our clothes. With one swift pull, my lips were a breath from his.

His voice was barely a whisper. The words slid out of his mouth like vipers, "I could kill you."

My eyes were locked on his and didn't waiver. "But you won't. You need me. The only reason you're still alive is that ward—my ward protecting you. You need me. I need you. We're forced to deal with each other."

Eric's eyes tore me apart thread by thread. I unraveled in his arms. I saw myself as he saw me—cruel, deceitful, and vindictive. The gaze would have undone me before. It would have twisted into my gut and made me double over, but now—now it lingered in the back of my mind like a wind stripped of its power. It simply brushed against my thoughts. It was a fact. It was a piece of information no more substantial than anything else. Eric's breath washed over me. His fingers pressed into my neck, making it throb.

Eric hesitated, seemingly frozen or unwilling to take the memories. My tongue pressed to the back of my teeth as my jaw tensed. He still didn't move. "Do it. Take what you need," I said through gritted teeth.

Without another word, Eric's lips smashed down on mine. The grip on the back of my neck tightened as his fingers pressed painfully into my skull. I didn't writhe, I didn't cry out. I forced myself to relax in his arms, as his lips pressed mine so hard that he cut my lip against my tooth. The taste of blood filled my mouth. Eric's other hand had grabbed my waist, as his fingers pressed hard enough to bruise my pale skin. I didn't move. I didn't scream. I made Eric what he was. It was my fault. As the words echoed in my mind, I no longer felt the power of their pain. It just was—a fact—like any other. I took his life. I ended him. He is what is, because of me. And I could accept it.

I felt my body go soft in his pressing hands. My lips parted as the kiss intensified. I didn't make him force me. I said I'd offer him what he needed and I intended to keep my word, but his kiss… It changed. Eric's fingers no longer pressed into me like he wanted to crush me. The intense hatred that initially pushed his lips to mine faded, as he brushed his tongue past my lips. I could taste him and thoughts of sweet shy Eric rushed to the front of my mind. The hand that was crushing my waist released me, and Eric's hand slowly, carefully moved higher until it rested on my cheek.

Eric released me from the kiss. He pulled back enough so our lips weren't intertwined, but our faces were still touching. I could still feel his warm, silky breath slide across my skin. His voice scraped as he spoke between jagged breaths, "What were you just thinking of?"

I kept my cheek pressed to his face, so I couldn't see his eyes. Eyes that damned me with every glance. Eyes that reflected exactly what I was. My heart was racing in my chest and I wondered when that started. I felt relaxed. Nearly indifferent. Nearly. "You. The way you were… before I changed you. Quiet. Sweet. Shy." My voice trailed off. His hand was still clutching the side of my face gently. It slid away like he could no longer bear to hold on. I moved away from him and coughed, refusing to look at him. An awkward silence lingered until I finally asked, "Did you get everything?"

He looked at me and laughed. It was a rich sound, like the laughs that used to come from him and not the bitter version that plagued him now. "No. One kiss can't take every memory. How long does it take to retell a story? To capture every detail? There are ten-thousand years of memories inside of your head. One kiss won't unlock all of them." He paused, looking away. The smile vanished, and the tension flowed back into his shoulders and down his arms. Seriousness overcame his features, "And we're running out of time. Some of the images are getting hazy. Some of the memories, I can't quite access." He shook his head, "Did I get everything?" My jaw tightened as my face felt hot. I refused to look at him, but he moved in front of me, his jaw agape. "Holy shit! Are you blushing?" he laughed.

At times I think that I was just made wrong. What could possibly make me blush? And it was Eric. I didn't like him. I didn't feel anything, but when his lips were on mine… I don't know. I was too numb to know.

Eric was suddenly serious, waiting and watching me. The red ran off of my cheeks. I glanced at him and away again, refusing to think more about it. Or what it meant. "How many times?" I asked.

"How much do you trust me?" he asked and nodded with a smirk on his face. "Everything isn't exactly floating to the surface. I have to find it. It's like stumbling through the darkness trying to find a piece of coal. It doesn't shine. It has no color. The only way to find it is to grab it with your hands. And your mind is a maze. My memories are hidden beneath layers of thick sludge, because you don't trust me. It makes the memories harder to find. Your mind is a labyrinth with things hiding in every corner." He swallowed and looked away, "And even when I do find my memories, it doesn't feel like they're my memories. Not anymore. They aren't attached to me any longer. I have to sort through everything to find what I'm looking for."

Glancing away from him, I nodded. "Fine. So, it'll take a while is what you're saying? You can't grab everything until we both trust each other." He opened his mouth to deny it, but snapped it shut again when I arched my eyebrow at him and said, "Really? You're going to deny it has anything to do with you. It's not just me, Eric. Trust takes two people, not one. Memories will flow freely when we trust each other."

Pressing my eyes closed, I leaned forward and pushed my hair out of my face uttering, "Which will be never."

CHAPTER TWENTY

Eric's hand pressed against the page to flatten it out. "I would have killed you that night, if I knew the page was missing." I'd torn the page with my pendant on it out of his book. When he opened it later, he was irate. That was why he came looking for me—to retrieve the page. But things didn't go as Eric planned. Somehow I overpowered him. There was fear hidden behind his eyes. He was no longer certain that he had the upper hand.

I glared at him. "Likewise." I bit my lip, not wanting to rehash that evening. "Can you read it?" I watched him, expecting him to read the entire page and then lie to me.

His eyes slipped over the page and back to my face. "I can, but I don't know what it means. I no longer have the memories that go with making these notations." He pointed to the ink drawing of my pendant. "This is the Kreturic pendant. It's the necklace around your neck." His gaze darted to my throat where the necklace hung. "It's made from the bones of angel wings and brimstone, and… "

My lips pulled away from my teeth in repulsion. I lifted the pendant off the hollow of my throat. "The white part—the flower is—it's… angel bones?" My mouth hung open, mortified.

Eric's eyebrow pulled up, "Yeah, so? Angels have power. Every piece of them has power. That pendant has power because of what it's made of. I just don't know exactly what kind of power it has, or how to use it." He gazed at the page. Pointing to the hurried script surrounding the edge he said, "These don't make sense to me." Black glyphs lined the page. There were no ink splotches. The only way I could tell that Eric had written it hastily was the lack of precision—the lines turned downward and didn't have the perfection of the rest of his notes. "This is saying that the pendant is tied to Kreturus—that's where the name came from. But this word here," he pointed to something that looked like scribbles, "isn't right. It shouldn't be that word." His finger tapped the page.

Turning my face up, and away from the page, I glanced at him. "What word is it?" I asked.

He looked up at me, irritated. "*Gloslos*. It's plural. But it should be singular." His jaw twitched. He hated speaking to me. Eric chewed his bottom lip with his jaw locked tight. He finally asked, "Is it possible I wrote this wrong? Is it possible that the old me, would have written the wrong word?" He stared at me.

I cast my gaze down at the book, and then back up at Eric, shaking my head. "I seriously doubt it. You were meticulous with everything. Nothing was out of place. Everything was… perfect." My head shook slowly, side to side. "That's not a mistake. Even if you were writing quickly, you would have chosen the most succinct word possible. You weren't one for wasting words."

Eric nodded, and his amber eyes shifted back to the creased page. "If it's plural, it means something I can't fathom. It changes the word to something that I don't know. So it's not that there are two of something. It more like the difference between a drop of water and the ocean. They are the same, but they aren't. And there is no way to know what I'm looking for when I search your mind." He ran his fingers through his hair, and then slapped the table hard, and turned away. He exhaled hard. "I can't even tell you what to think to try and pull the memory forward. Without understanding this page, I'm searching though millions of memories totally blind. They aren't even merged with your memories. There's no point of reference to tell me anything." He shook his head. "I may not find it."

I saw the slope of his shoulders, and the tension between his eyes. There was nothing he could do. Looking for a lost memory was like trying to find a speck of dust in the snow. Staring at the page, I curled my fingers, pulling it closer to my face. Finally, I asked, "Will you read it to me? The whole thing?" I studied the page, running my fingers over each carefully crafted character before smoothing it onto the table.

Eric's face pinched tightly as he looked back at me. "What for?" he asked. "You can't understand it."

Turning, I looked up at him, still resting my fingers on the page. "Then explain it to me. Translate. Tell me what this says in its entirety."

The bottom of Eric's lip twitched, but he returned to the table. His tapered fingers slid across the old parchment, pointing as he did so. He read, explaining that there were three quadrants to the page. They were in a specific order. The language was neither Greek nor Latin, but something of a code that Eric had created using a combination of both languages. It kept others from reading his notes. The quadrants were separated by a notation. On this page, the notation was the drawing.

He twisted the page as he read, translating it to me. "The pendant will seek its owner. There is no stasis. It's living and needs contact with its entity. The pendant," he paused looking up at me while his pointer finger pressed on the parchment, "this word is written to infer plurality—which makes no sense—so I'm reading it singular. The pendant was used during the last angel demon war." Eric twisted the page. The letters looked to be upside down, but he read on. "Comprised of angel bones, wings according to the legend, and brimstone, the pendant will remain dormant, asleep until awakened." He pointed to the words encircling the picture, "These are describing it—there are two intertwined flowers nestled together. Blood ignites the charm when the pendant, plural, is needed." He twisted the page again. "Use varies by user, power, and ability. Cost. Question mark." He looked up at me, as if to say, see I told you that you wouldn't understand. "Any epiphany, Taylor?"

I frowned at him, grabbing the page and studying the lines that made no sense. "No," I admitted, "but how could it not help? At the very least, the stuff written on this page will be floating at the forefront of my mind now. If you tried to take the memories now, would you be able to?"

He shrugged. "I don't know. I don't know if it works like that. I have no idea how it works. You're…"

"Stop talking," I said, grabbing the front of his shirt. He tensed, ready to shirk me off. I yanked the fabric in my hands, pulling him closer. "The more we say, the more this stuff slips into the back of my mind again."

His jaw tensed. Two golden eyes burned into me like the summer sun. His hands reached for my waist, jerked me closer in one swift motion that closed the gap between us. And he kissed me. He hated it. He hated every moment of pressing his lips to mine. He hated that I didn't respond the way that he did. He hated that my anger was repressed, or masked, or hidden so deeply within me that he couldn't touch it. He wanted to evoke a response. He wanted to make me writhe, in pain or ecstasy—but to respond to his touch. To him. It was my reaction that calmed him in the past; my fear and anger. He wanted me to experience agony like him. But I didn't. Now it was gone, nowhere to be seen.

After a moment, Eric's kissed softened, and his fingers that pressed into me relaxed, like before. I felt the black cloud he was searching as his tongue swept against mine. He pushed through the memories, the remnants of his former life that still lived within me. There was so much, but I never felt any part of it. The residue from his former life was invisible to me before this. I didn't even know it was there. But now, now I could sense it like an eyelash resting softly my cheek. The only way to know it's even there is for something else to brush up against it. And that's what Eric was doing. His mind swam through the memories as if he were gently blowing an eyelash away. The sensations lingered at the back of mind, echoing with the lust conjured by his blood. My body knew he was there and wanted to respond, but my mind wouldn't allow it. The emotional response, the need for him, was disconnected.

But, then the distance faded, silently falling to the background, and the only thing I could feel was him. Eric. Eric kissing me. Eric's arms around me. Eric's scent, his taste, his touch on my body. The lust that burned through me last time he'd fed me his blood tore through my stomach like a burst of flame. The connection re-established itself. I could feel him. I wanted him. My heart exploded, shattering into a million pieces, all equally starved for his touch.

Horror raced through my veins, and I tore away from him, wide eyed. "What'd you do?" The words flew out of my mouth in a rushed panic. My clothes clung to me. My skin glistened. It was so damn hot.

Eric studied me before he spoke. His gaze slipped over my body taking in the sheen on my skin, the pounding heart inside my chest, and the jagged breaths that were too shallow. Too uneven. His lips curled up at the corners, as he folded his arms across his chest. "Nothing. I found the memories from the time that page was written, but you pulled away before I could make sense of it." He watched me for a moment. And in that moment the connection between his blood and my mind sizzled like an electrical wire downed from a storm, erratically coming into contact and burning anything around it. I pressed my hands to my head, pulling away from him, but his fingers didn't release my waist. He watched the turmoil play out as my frantic mind tried to connect with my emotions.

I blinked once, feeling hot, when a dark haze clouded my vision and started to pull me down. My face slowly lowered to the table, pulling out of Eric's grasp as I fell, but I didn't stop there. The downward thrust pulled me so hard. My head felt so heavy. It was as if a sandbag had been tied to each curl. The weight was too much. I couldn't stop myself from falling forward. My heart raced, pounding against my ribs as my cheek pressed against the cold floor. Eric stood over me watching me.

Her voice was in my mind, calling me. The Demon Princess was beckoning me, pulling me into the vision. I tried to speak, but the words didn't fall out. Breathing softly, I stared at Eric with my lips parted. His hands were pressed into his pockets. His head was lowered, watching me with wonder, not moving to help. Not a trace of concern on his face. As my eyes flickered shut, a soft smile lined his lips, and then everything was gone.

CHAPTER TWENTY-ONE

"You've been avoiding me, little one." Her voice was cold. She was cold. She stood next to me, casting a glance down over my shoulder. "After our last lesson, I thought you'd be eager for more."

I repressed every urge I had. There was no other way to survive this. Pressing my eyes closed, I felt my heart racing in my chest. I sucked in a slow breath and ignored it. The tension flowed out of my body as she began again without waiting. She spoke, and I did as she said. It was the bargain. This was what I asked for. These things, they were the things that I'd wanted to know. But as she taught me, I saw the horror in Collin's eyes all over again.

She was speaking, saying words that fell flat from her bored lips, "It is called Hellsfire or Hellsflame. You can call it. It has the power of fire, plus a little kick. It can destroy. It can kill." She moved past me, her dress swirling as she turned to look back at me. Her gloved hands were delicately placed together in front of her abdomen. She wore the cloak with the hood that covered her completely. There wasn't a drop of light within that hood. The only thing I could see were a pair indigo eyes shining from within.

"And the price?" I asked, before she failed to tell me. Again. She never told me anything. She just wanted me to do it. But not this time. Conjuring something from the Underworld, something lethal, had to have a hefty premium.

She turned toward me, the heels of her boots click-clacking against the stone floor. She stopped in front of me. Locoicia appeared lifeless, not breathing, not moving as she stopped in front of me. Blood rushed through my ears in a loud hiss, and my pulse quickened. The woman placed her hands together lightly, and pulled them to her chin. Her ruby lips twisted into a false smile, "Did you wish to only learn bits and pieces of things from me, or was that not what we bargained for?" My mouth cracked open to speak, but her hands flew apart—one dropping to her side and, as she stepped toward me, pressed the other to my lips silencing me. "No. I know exactly what our bargain was. I teach you everything I know. Part of that, dear girl," she lowered her gloved finger and turned away, "is learning to deal with the price—even if it is greater than you imagined." She pressed the palms of her hands together, and kept her gaze on her hands. She didn't turn to me. There was no explanation. No information. No price given. "Call it. Call the Hellsfire into your palm. Do as I say or you break your word, and I collect my price."

My body was already weary. She didn't have sapphire serum in her chest. It didn't matter that no one could see it. It didn't matter that she insulated the poison so I could use dark magic—I still felt it. It still took its toll. And I was already tired. Eric's kiss had already drained me. It seemed as he stole back his memories, he also took some of my energy.

Pressing my lips together, I knew I had no choice. The only way out of this was to move forward. Tired or not. I did as she said. Uttering the words clearly in my mind, I focused my unblinking gaze on my open palm. This felt so similar to calling light, but it had a more sinister twisted edge to it. Hellsfire was more potent than regular fire. It didn't burn itself out. It never stopped burning, so calling it was insane. You had to know exactly what to do with it and how to get rid of it once you were through using it. Trying to swallow back the lump in my throat, I felt the heat form in my hand. I glanced up at Locoicia to see if she would tell me to stop, but she did not. As I stood there, liquid fire poured from nowhere into the center of my palm. It splashed down, licking tongues of blue and white flames as it slid its snakelike coils into my palm.

A scream erupted unexpectedly from my lips. The flesh on my hand was being melted away by the Hellsfire. I could feel every lick of pain registering in my mind with utter clarity. It wasn't the faint echo of a disconnected thought. The pain was a loud gong of affirmation. My ability to feel pain wasn't hushed. The Hellsflame burned through it, and was melting the skin of my palm as I watched in terror. Stray hairs clung to my glistening face as I looked up to the Demon Princess for help. But she did not speak. Her eyes did not waiver. She wanted me to hold onto the flame. If I released it, she would only make me do it again, so I held on.

Twisting tongues of fire danced in my hand, hissing and searing as they moved. Clutching my arm with my other hand, I held it in place. No screams poured through me. The only sign of stress were the beads of sweat rolling down my temples, leaving a cool trail in their wake. The pain of the Hellsflame burrowed deep down into the bones of my hand. The fires found the tiny bones in my fingers and multiplied over and over again, until the pain and the heat was so intense that I thought my bones would shatter from within. When I felt my body begin to slump from the sapphire serum, the hooded woman stepped forward, and grabbed the flame from my hands. It extinguished in a puff of smoke.

Breathing hard, I fell to one knee. There was bitter disappointment in her voice when she spoke, "I thought we were past this." She sighed, and flicked her wrist. My body spasmed in pain, but I bit my lip so I wouldn't cry out. "Why would you possibly negate your apathy?" The flick of her wrist flashed again, and I fell to my other knee. My teeth bit down hard, too hard, drawing blood from my lip. She stepped towards me. "Must I keep teaching you this lesson? Have you not learned it yet? Do I really have to take you within a breath of death to make you realize what you have to do! This is not a game, little one. You cannot defeat Kreturus without learning this lesson!" She flicked her wrist again. Pain coursed through me, and I didn't understand. I didn't understand why I felt her lashes on my back. I didn't comprehend why I could feel my skin rip apart slowly, bit by bit. My eyes pressed closed tightly, trying to endure the pain. My mind searched for the connection, desperately seeking to sever it again. But it came back. My feelings returned. And I didn't know why.

Raw screams ripped out of my throat, rushing past gritted teeth as she lashed me again and again. This time when she finished my back, she twisted me around and flick by flick, she lashed my entire torso. Every inch of my middle was raw and gushing blood. Finally, when she was done, I laid still with my face pressed to the cold stone floor feeling nothing. My eyes stared blankly as no thought or pain registered in my mind. My lips were cracked, and parted. Breaths that were too small entered my body. I could not fight back. I could not allow her to win. Slick red blood clung to my cheek and caked in my hair. Illeca sat at the table with her legs crossed, looking down at me with contempt.

"It was for your own good," she said. I did not answer. I did not move. "You'll die when you fight him if you feel anything. Your senses are the first thing he'll use against you. There isn't anything he won't do. There is nothing he won't try. And Kreturus will do everything within his power to utterly destroy you. That is why we must do it first." She stared at me, lying in a pool of my own blood. She sighed and looked away, disgusted. "Go. Go home, little one. Do not return to me again until you have healed."

My eyes fell shut, and the world was no more.

CHAPTER TWENTY-TWO

It felt like there were bricks on top of my chest. It was as if someone were adding them one by one. I tried to breathe, but it was so hard. Words whispered in my ear, and arms around my back made me wince. I couldn't help it. I wasn't able to disconnect myself completely. Trying to call the Hellsflame showed her that I couldn't. It didn't matter what the reason was. Nothing mattered in that moment.

Pressure moved slowly across my forehead. Fingers were pressing against my brow. My eyelids felt like one piece. They would not separate. My mind slipped back, away from the voice—away from the pain. The darkness surrounded me, but the voice called.

It spoke my name, "Ivy. Ivy. Ivy," like the drip of a faucet. It called softly. Over and over again. The voice didn't rest. The hand on my brow didn't stop. "Ivy. Ivy. Ivy."

I slipped away into dreams that held no release. Pain still caused my bones to ache, and my body to tremble. "Ivy," the voice called. And this time, I peeled back my eyes and saw him. Eric. Eric sitting on my bed in the old church. A wet cloth was in his hand, and he was dabbing my forehead, and softly speaking. "That's a good girl. Come on, now. Open your eyes. You can't leave yet, Ivy. We're not done. That's right, Ivy… Open those eyes. Come on."

I tried to swallow, but my throat burned. My tongue was thick. Tired eyes gazed at Eric. I didn't speak. I couldn't speak.

"There you are," he said softly, looking down at me. He wiped the wet cloth across my head, gently dabbing it as he went. "So, you decided to come back after all?" he smiled, but it faded from his lips too fast. The hatred was hidden. I couldn't see it in his eyes and it didn't exist in his touch. Eric pressed the towel into a bowl of water on the table next to my bed, and twisted it in his hands. Water trickled out of the cloth and back into the bowl. Then he pressed it to my searing flesh again.

"Eric?" I moaned.

His eyes locked onto mine. They were like big gold coins, perfectly round. "Don't speak. I don't know what happened to you, but something beat the hell out of you. I thought you weren't gonna wake up. You're covered in… I don't know, but you're still bleeding. There are welts all over you." He lifted the wet cloth from my face, and placed it in the bowl. As he soaked it with water and rung it out, he hesitated, leaving his hands over the bowl. He didn't look back at me. "I remember this, from before." His voice was different, distant. "You on the forest floor, crying in my arms when you woke up. But this time, you didn't wake up." He turned toward me. Eric's eyes slid over my face to my torso. He pressed his eyes closed, then looked at my face again. "This time, you bled as you laid there. You screamed. It was as if someone was… " his words trailed off. His voice was angry, "Who did this?"

Lowering my eyelids, I blinked once slowly. My mouth felt like it had to move miles to open enough to form words. "I can't tell you." My throat was parched and scraping as I tried to speak. Eric stiffened. His eyes moved away from me, his face wouldn't look at me. I tried to lift my hand to get his attention. I would have placed it on top of his. I would have said things, but it was all I could do to raise a finger. He saw, and turned his head back to me. "I did something… I made a blood bargain. Otherwise," I rasped, "I'd tell you."

Eric took a deep breath, and pressed two fingers to the pinched place between his eyes. When he looked back at me, I saw something flicker within their depths. Something that made me feel safe. He cleared his throat, "I can heal most of these. You would have been able to do it yourself, but whoever did this to you pushed you too far. Ivy, do you understand? They would have killed you if I wasn't here. I took your half dead body and carried you into your room."

"Like before," I whispered, trying to suppress a moan. My body felt like it had been torn to bits and someone stapled me back together. There wasn't a single place on me that wasn't in total agony, and my mind knew this even if I didn't feel it completely.

"Hmm? What do you mean?" he asked. Eric watched my face, trying to remember something he no longer knew.

My eyelids crept lower, masking my eyes from his curious gaze. "Like before." The world went black.

———

When I awoke, I felt different. Like the walls that held my emotions back were re-erected and firmly in place. My body throbbed, but it was a distant echo in the back of my mind. Eric was lying next to me, watching me, as my eyes fluttered opened. For a long time, I didn't move or speak.

He finally broke the silence. "Feel better?"

"Yes. And no." I turned my head slowly to look at him. Eric was lying on his side, next to me on my bed. Sheets and extra blankets were draped across my body. A lamp was emitting a soft glow from across the room. The light drifted across his face, highlighting his features. This was the room that had been mine when I lived with Al earlier in the year. In Eric's hands, he held the corner of a blanket. He was twisting the corner into a tiny spire. I sat up slowly, pressing my fingers to my body. I raised my bare arm, holding it out in front of me, turning it over and seeing nothing but smooth skin. All the scars Locoicia gave me were gone.

He nodded, glancing at me from the corner of his eyes. "You're stronger than you were. Stronger than most. Every inch of your body was covered in lacerations that cut through the muscle and went down to the bone. Did you piss the demon off? Or were you doing something you shouldn't have?"

My lips were dry. My mouth was dry, but they were facts. Statements. I shook my head in response. "No, I was supposed to learn something. Something that I failed to learn last time." I couldn't look at him. Tugging at the sheets, I pulled them closer to my neck. My shredded clothes didn't cover me, and I could feel the remains of my shirt and jeans trying to slip off of me. They were hard, and covered in dried blood that was stabbing into my skin.

"Did you learn it this time?" he asked. His eyes caressed the side of my face, as he spoke. I nodded. "Good." He paused, and several moments passed when he spoke again. "We don't have much time left. I need the rest of those memories before they fade, or we won't be able to go after the Satan's Stone." He watched me for a moment. When he spoke again, his voice was… different. "Why make a blood bargain?"

I stared straight ahead. As I spoke I could feel the passionless words slip out of my mouth, "I have to kill him. Kreturus can't win." Turning, I searched his face for understanding, but was only met with a blank stare. "He can't win."

Eric pushed himself up onto one elbow. "Get dressed. Your clothes are… beyond repair. There's still stuff that's yours in that closet." He looked down, his hair blocking his face.

I turned back to look at Eric, lying on his side looking everywhere else, but not at me. "Why'd you heal me?" The pain price he paid for healing me made my skin crawl. I didn't want him to do anything for me, and yet, he did.

His hair was tousled. There were dark circles under his eyes. Eric kept his gaze on the blanket. Pressing his lips together, he finally spoke, "I don't know." His face shot up, and he glared at me with an intensity that made my stomach twist. Minutes passed. When he finally spoke again he said, "I could have. But, someone else…" he shook his head and looked away. "They took what was mine. I watched as you were sucked into the nightmare. Your body lay before me and each wound slowly opened and bled. I watched. I did nothing to stop it. Nothing to call you back." The place between his eyes was pinched tightly. "Your body writhed, as you were ripped apart. I thought it'd be enough to watch. I thought it'd be enough to see you in pain, to see you squirming in agony for what you did to me. But, it wasn't. I was supposed to be the one to do that to you."

Horror spidered through my veins, spinning inside of me so quickly it was all that I could do to sit perfectly still and listen. I should have wanted to throw back the blankets and run. But there was an eerie calmness that held me in place. "But you didn't do that to me. You weren't the one who tortured me. It was someone else. So, what then?" His gaze lifted and rested on my face. Golden eyes peered from under his brow. Expressionless. "You've decided… what?"

"I've decided nothing," he jumped up, off the bed, and away from me. "Nothing's changed. But no one else will kill you. If you die, it'll be by my hand and no one else's." His arms folded over his chest as he moved away from me and toward the door. He reached for the knob, and slipped through the door without another word.

CHAPTER TWENTY-THREE

After showering and dressing, I walked through the church with wet hair. It felt like icicles clung to my head and rested on my shoulders. I suppressed a shiver. When I entered the nave, I walked past rows of pews and saw Eric sitting silently staring at the glass again. I didn't conceal my presence this time, but he didn't turn or acknowledge me until I was at his shoulder.

"Why hasn't he come?" Eric pushed his hands on the wooden altar and twisted himself around toward me. It was a question that I'd been dreading.

I glanced at him once, and walked past him to sit on the floor. I folded my legs under me and said, "He's not coming."

"Why's that?" Eric leaned forward, suddenly very interested. His eyes were razor sharp watching every movement, every twitch of my tongue, every flinch of my fingers.

I gazed at him, wondering if I should say anything about Collin. It felt like my life was a shard of glass that was meant for something else, but the fragments had become so small that I had no idea what it was supposed to be anymore. Collin turning on me was just another splinter of glass that made no sense. The confession rolled around in my mind before I spoke. My voice as flat, "The bond is broken. The connection between us isn't what it was. It seems impaired, if not completely gone. It's regressing. Fading into a void."

Eric stared at me. "And how did it break? A soul bond is much stronger than any blood bond, and I'm not entirely convinced that I have no effect on you any longer." His eyes moved over my lingering on my lips as he did so. A smile snaked across his mouth, "Which means that he still must have a hold of you, too."

My hands clenched in my lap as eyes narrowed to slits. I glared at him. "You do not have a hold on me. Your blood doesn't tempt me at all."

He slid off the altar and walked slowly towards me. With each step he spoke, "And why would that be? What did your demon possibly tell you to do to break your lust for me?" My gaze was on the floor. His arrogant tone made me want to punch him in the face. "Or was it intentional at all?"

Shit. He knows. He knows that he has no effect on me because I can't feel the lust. It is still there, whispering in the back of my mind, but I no longer care because I don't feel the compulsion to act on my feelings. He stopped. Eric's sneaker clad foot rested on the floor in front of me.

Through gritted teeth, I muttered, "What's your point?"

He knelt down. Eric's face was directly in front of mine. His eyes drifted over my face, landing on my lips, "Taylor, my point is," his gaze raised to my eyes, "that your bond with him isn't broken. It's subdued. It's been muffled. Muted. But, it still exists." He rose and turned away from me. His feet tracked back to the altar where he jumped up, and slid back, dangling his legs off the side. Eric folded his fingers in his lap. "You can deny your lust for my blood the same way you can deny his bond with you. It's still within you, but you no longer feel the need to respond." He waited for me to answer, to affirm his declarations, but I didn't. He already knew he was right. He was always right.

Swallowing hard, I asked, "So?" Patches of light formed shards of colors that scattered across the floor. There was no pattern.

Air rushed out of his lungs in a harsh laugh. "You are… " he turned his head to the side, "completely naive." My neck snapped up. A smile had twisted across his face. Two eyes sparkled in place of his normal glare. He leaned forward, watching me. Waiting for me to deny the words that fell from his lips. My jaw twitched. I scowled at him, waiting for him to speak. His voice was smooth, and completely confident, "He's using you. Collin could find you whenever he wanted. But he doesn't. He didn't come last night, and he's not coming now." Eric watched me from under his brow. He lowered his voice, as if Collin might be near, listening to us. "He's waiting. Waiting for you."

My jaw hung open. Eric sounded insane. "He is not using me," I snapped jumping to my feet. My body was lined with tension. Anger boiled somewhere in the recesses of my mind. Like a string tickling my arm, I swatted at the burning emotion and caught it. The rage coursed through me, violently beating in my heart. Before I knew it I was snarling in front of him, and looking up into his smug face. "Collin left me. That's why he's not here. He's not waiting for a damn thing."

Eric's smile widened, "Hmm. Indeed. He's not using you. He cares about you, but he left you with some deranged demon to slice off your skin down to your bones, and then he allowed your worst enemy to watch over you while you healed. That would be me, in case you missed it." His brow pinched together as he hissed in my face. "I am the one who wanted to do that to you. I am the one who wanted to see you suffer in so much agony that you died. Me," he breathed. Leaning back, the anger unpinched his face. Eric's eyes flicked over my body, then back to some distant spot to the left. "Sure," he muttered, "That makes sense. That's what'd I do if I wanted to protect someone I loved, too."

"The bond broke," I snapped. The muscles in my neck constricted as I spoke, "He couldn't feel it. And he didn't know who I was with or what she was doing. He doesn't know I'm with you or that he could have lost me last night. He doesn't know!"

The smile melted off his face. He leaned forward slightly, resting his elbows on his knees. "But I can still feel you—and our bloodbond isn't very strong. I sense you, like I sense myself. You were able to sneak up on me the other day, because you were hidden from me. You masked your blood." His eyes connected with mine and wouldn't let go. His voice resonated with reason that I couldn't accept. "Soul bonds do not work like that. There is no hiding. You know it's true. Ivy. He still feels you, and yet... He. Did. Not. Come." His lips formed around each word, slowly enunciating the facts.

Shaking my head, I stepped back. "He would have come. He would have. Collin wouldn't have done that.

No." The pitch of my voice rose the longer I spoke. "He couldn't feel my pain. He didn't know… " The words felt like barbs of wire being pulled out my throat.

The certainty on Eric's face was plain. "Say what you want, but I think he's manipulating you. His side of the bond is still there. He still knows where you are and what you're doing. He chose not to come. He chose to let you die."

"You're wrong," I growled, and turned on my foot to storm out the front door.

CHAPTER TWENTY-FOUR

Before I realized where I was going, I found myself standing outside the high school. It was after the last bell had rung. The parking lots were nearly empty, except for a few stragglers. I stood in the snow looking at the building, wondering if Eric's words were true when a familiar voice spoke from behind me.

"He isn't here," she said, her voice lacking its normal perkiness. Jenna Marie stepped next to me in a pink parka and fuzzy white boots. The faux fur lining her hood encircled her face, with each individual strand of synthetic hair moving in the wind. "He's not been here for a while now." Golden hair cascaded from under a pink woolen cap to her shoulders, and down her back.

I nodded, staring at her somber face. She was a Martis. One of Al's oldest friends. The perky pink girl was Al's mentor. But everything about her was wrong. The angle of her shoulders, the smoothness of her steps, the line of her lips. She seemed sad. There was only one reason for that. I turned to her and asked, "You know? About Al?"

She nodded, her glassy eyes looking to the side, away from me. "Yes, I know." She swallowed while looking at a snowdrift that lined the end of the circle drive in front of the school. When she spoke again, her voice was clear and strong. "Al knew Eric would be her death when she found him. She saw it in a vision. So did I. Al raised him anyway. She played her part," Jenna Marie turned her face back towards me, "and it's time you played yours." I opened my mouth to speak, but she shushed me. I bristled, but was quiet. "Collin Smith is one of them. His power rivals most demons, yet he is a Valefar. He has a soul—partly his own, partly yours." Her blue eyes held sympathy, but also courage and conviction that I didn't know she had. "You and he are fighting for different sides, and yet here you stand, looking for him." She paused, looking at me with a slight tilt to her head. "Why?"

I started to walk away. "I don't have to explain myself to you, Martis. There are no sides in this battle. Only living and dying."

She reached out and wrapped her slender fingers around my arm, stopping me. "That's where you're wrong." She laughed. Her voice was deep, her blue eyes like ice, "You are so incredibly wrong. This is more than life or death. It's utter annihilation. Don't stand there and think you know more than me."

Twisting out of her grip, I shook her off, "I don't have to listen to you. Martis are all the same self-serving corrupt immortals who are high on power. Go play with Julia and leave me alone." I spit the words at her, not expecting her to react. Martis pride was one thing. The way Jenna Marie reacted was another.

She laughed one short laugh that made her body lurch forward. Her blonde hair fell over her shoulders. Snow clung to her cute hat making her look like a Barbie doll. She was always perfect. Rosy cheeks, golden hair, and a perfect smile. "So, we'll do this the hard way, then." She reached out and grabbed me. And I realized, a second too late, that I completely underestimated her.

CHAPTER TWENTY-FIVE

A blinding light faded and when my eyes refocused we were standing in the same place, but everything was muted—the color, the sounds, the falling snow. And nothing moved. It was as if time had stopped. Nearly snapping my neck off, I twisted toward Jenna Marie— the girl I didn't know. The girl who held more power than I thought possible. My stomach felt as if I'd eaten a bucket of nails. With my mouth hanging open, I slipped my foot backwards, away from her. Uncertain of everything now.

As my head swiveled around, I took in the gray snow that had been brilliant white, and the light gray building that had been red brick. Snowflakes hung suspended in the air in front of us. My breath had frozen and hung in the air where I'd been standing. It was no longer cold, but it wasn't warm. The biting winter wind was frozen with the snowflakes, neither moving or howling. It no longer caught our hair and thrust it with its unseen fingers.

Jeanna Marie repeated herself, "You do not know more than me." Her voice was tense. Her delicate arms were folded over her fluffy coat.

Finally finding my voice, I said, "You're not one of them, are you? You're not a Martis at all."

She shook her head. Jenna Marie's eyes were strange. It was as if they were made of water and gemstones—smooth and so clear that I should have been able to look into her skull. But her eyes had become gray and the only thing I saw was my own reflection. "You think that we'd leave you here to destroy everything in one act of complete stupidity. Angels wouldn't do that! I could kill that boy! He shouldn't have saved you. But then, Kreturus shouldn't have been out. It made using the stone pointless." She shook her head, as if she was dislodging an unwanted memory.

There were so many things that I wanted to latch onto. But I bit my tongue, and when she stopped speaking I asked, "The stone? You used the Satan's Stone?" My eyebrows rose as I stepped towards her.

A rushed breath of air released from her lungs. "I can't pull off this Stasis for much longer. I can only hold time still for a short while. It's incredibly draining, but you are about to make another mistake. Listen, Ivy. I'm an angel. I was there from the beginning. Before you, before Al, and before Kreturus. I'm one of the ancient ones, the oldest of our kind. I have more power in my pinky than you have in your whole body. You need to know—you're a pawn in this whole thing." As her pink shimmering lips moved she spoke at a hurried pace. "You were in the wrong place at the wrong time, but it's too late to free you from this. Too many things were set into motion that can't be undone. I did not use the stone. Another angel did. He paid the price and died because of it. Satan's Stone destroys as it grants power." Her lashes lowered as she looked to the gray snow-covered earth, "Lorren gave his life to use it during the first war. And everything stopped. The war ended. Demons and angels alike, dropped their weapons, and left. There was peace for a long time— until Kreturus. Until that demon raised his head and started the war over again. But this time, it was more violent than the last. This time, he wouldn't be stopped. Another angel sacrificed himself. He aided the Martis in trapping Kreturus in that hole in Hell. We lost two of our best warriors trying to defeat the demons. The price of the stone is death, Ivy. You cannot use it." She glared at me with her bewitched eyes. Her pale skin had taken on a slight shimmer as she spoke. Passion laced her voice as she tried to convince me to stop looking for something that couldn't save me. But it only made me more interested in the Satan's Stone.

"An angel used the stone, and died to stop the demons both times?" She nodded. "The solider, the angelic warrior who stopped the first war by holding up the Satan's Stone—his name was Lorren?"

She nodded again, "Yes, and he died. His wings were stripped off his back as he was smashed to bits. Nothing remained of him. And no one remembered him." Her expression shifted, looking past me to the horizon as if she could see something that I could not. Her eyes didn't blink. "Lorren was the warrior who held up the stone." Her eyes pressed closed. Long lashes swept against her cheeks.

A million questions raced through my mind, but there was no time. "Lorren? Tall, young, thin Lorren? Lorren with black hair, a snarky mouth, and an affinity for healing?" Her eyes flicked open, wide. "That Lorren?"

She nodded. "The gate of the Underworld was named for him… I named it after him. To remember him by… "

"Ah," I said, "then I have some news for you." My lips turned up in a smile. "Lorren is alive."

CHAPTER TWENTY-SIX

Jeanna Marie's face was frozen, as still and unmoving as the snowflakes that were around us. "Did you hear me? He's not dead, Jenna Marie. Lorren is alive. He's the one who healed me, well, half healed me."

Her perfectly pink lips twitched as my words sunk in. She shook her head, "That can't be. An angel can't survive without his wings. The bones within the wings provide us with energy and... for lack of a better word—magic. They give us power, and provide us with life." Her head cocked to the side, "And I know what you are thinking. Mine are hidden, as are all of the angels' wings." She shook her head, "So there is no way that Lorren survived. He couldn't have. He can't. His wings were ripped off his body. The stone's price was his life."

"No," I shook my head, "the stone's price was his wings. Lorren is alive." I repeated myself, then added, "I don't care if you believe me or not. However, I do care about this place," I pointed to the school, "and the people who live here. I can't let Kreturus destroy this place. I can't. Tell me where the stone is Jenna Marie. Tell me where I can find Satan's Stone."

Still half dazed, she shook her head, "That's just it. The stone splits in two so it cannot be used. The second time we found it was a fluke. The second half turned up in the Underworld, of all places. The Guardian gave it to the angel who trapped Kreturus. That angel was the last to have the stone." She shook her head, "But I don't know who it was."

Stepping towards her, I asked, "Why not?" The snowflakes twitched as if they would start to fall again any second. "Why, not? How could you remember Lorren but not the second angel?"

The snow around us hissed as it began to fall again. The world came back into color as noise pelted my ears again, chasing away the silence. Jenna Marie didn't raise her downcast gaze when she spoke. Her pink lips turned into a faint smile. "Because Lorren was mine."

CHAPTER TWENTY-SEVEN

Jenna Marie stared at me as snow fell around us. Her face said she wanted to believe me, but there was something in the curve of her mouth that said something else. "Take me to him."

"I can't, not yet." I glanced at her and back at the school. "I need you to tell me something. You've been alive long enough to know the truth." She turned her gaze toward me, suddenly more interested. A lump formed in my throat. I didn't want to ask her. Part of me didn't want to know, but I had to know. "How old is Collin Smith?" She started to scold me, telling me to stay away from him, but I cut her off, "Just answer the question! If you were around so long, you would know.

The only other person helping me is a fucked up Valefar who'll rip my throat out when I least expect it! I need you to tell me. Tell me the truth. How old is he?"

Jenna Marie tilted her head to the side, and bit back a word or two. Snow clung to her hair in tiny pieces making the golden tresses sparkle like they held tiny diamonds. The snow didn't melt when it touched her. "Collin's young, less than a millennium. But that doesn't mean he's safe. There is no such thing as a safe Valefar."

"There's no such thing as a safe angel either," I said. Then before she could speak, I asked, "Why would he hide? Why would Lorren not want anyone to know he was alive?"

She shook her head. "I don't know."

CHAPTER TWENTY-EIGHT

The basement was empty. The props and backdrops draped the walls casting strange shapes across the narrow room. I padded across the darkness to the worn leather couch, and fell onto its thick cushions. I pressed my hands under the crooks in my arms, trying to warm them. I sat where he sat, where I'd found Collin so many times before. Oddly, we shared the same fondness of small dark spaces that tend to freak most people out. But for me, it provided four walls of safety and comfort. Collin came here when he needed to think, as did I.

Something called me to this place. I effonated inside without disturbing the sapphire serum in my chest, but I was feeling weaker. Locoicia said she removed the venom's mark and nothing more. I would still die if the poison remained buried in my chest. The toll of the poison did not go unnoticed. Drawing in air took effort, as it became harder and harder to force myself to breathe. I wanted to sleep. To close my eyes and dream, but I didn't dare. Awake I could resist Locoicia's calls. Awake, I could defend myself against Valefar, Martis, and misguided angels. The cement store room was four walls of peace.

I leaned back into the cushions, slouching and pushed my hair out of my face. Getting down here wasn't easy. Jenna Marie wouldn't leave. She insisted I take her to Lorren, but Lorren isn't part of my plan. The entire situation with Lorren bothered me. He's supposed to be dead and he lied to my face. Those were two serious issues that needed to be remedied. Nothing was as it seemed. No one was trustworthy. Not now. Not ever. Tilting my head back, I gazed at the rafters on the ceiling. They were sprayed with a chunky plaster compound that had collected a lifetime of dust.

His voice made me jump, "Have you reconsidered?" Collin stood across from me in the shadows. His hands were in his pockets. "Or are you still insisting on going through with it?" The tilt of his head, the gleam of his eye were confrontational. He came looking for me.

I didn't move. Thoughts slashed through my mind in a vortex or doubt. My eyes lingered on his lips for a beat too long, before they slid away to the floor, I said, "No. Have you reconsidered?"

He stepped towards me, blue eyes piercing into my soul, "I can't." His dark leather jacket clung to his body. The lapel was open, revealing a black shirt beneath.

"Neither can I," I answered. Collin's gaze shifted between my mouth and my eyes. I couldn't feel his thoughts. I couldn't sense his emotions. Rising, I walked toward him. His eyes dropped to my hips, taking in the gentle sway of my walk until I stopped in front of him. I resisted the urge to reach out and run my fingers across his cheeks. I resisted and asked, "Do you really think I'd kill you?"

His jaw tensed. "It's not whether you want to or not. It's what happens." Impossibly blue eyes locked with mine. "I have to tell you something." Looking up into his face, I wanted nothing more than to press my lips to his and melt in his arms. But I didn't move. He stepped forward, and tilted his forehead down, touching it to mine. His fingers tangled in my hair, as his breath washed across my lips in a rush. "I have to tell you… something." His words were barely audible.

My breath caught in his throat. I lifted my hands and placed them against his chest, touching the exposed skin at his throat just about his neckline. My finger traced along the edge of his shirt. "Tell me, then." My hands slid around to the bare skin at the base of his neck. It was the only chink in his armor, the only place where we could still feel each other.

His words brushed inside my mind, *It's not what you think. Nothing is.*

I don't understand, I replied watching him, waiting for more. Collin stood frozen in front of me. The bond was reduced to an ember of what it had been.

Collin's body twisted out of my grip, and the bond shattered. He stepped away, slipping out of my reach. "I have to go." His voice caught in his throat. His fingers stretched once, and relaxed. He looked away.

Blankly, I stared at him. A wave of intense emotions pelted into me before he released me. Staring at the smooth leather that followed the curve of his back, I watched him step away. The emotions that swam through the bond were vibrant and wild. They made no sense, but the main thing that startled me was the remorse that blared through everything else. It was so devastatingly thick that he could barely breathe. It was as if Collin couldn't force his body to breathe. It felt like the same thing that was happening to me, but much worse. The wire bands that restricted his chest made him feel trapped. There was nothing I could do. This is where we stood. I said nothing, as he turned to leave. There was nothing more to say. The heat surrounding him intensified and he effonated away leaving me alone in the darkness.

CHAPTER TWENTY-NINE

Anxiety laced my erratic movements. I shoved my hands in my pockets as I walked through the doors of the church and came to a screeching halt. Black scales lined the floors, strewn about as if they were confetti. My jaw dropped as I turned my head, taking in the scene. It was so bizarre. It was so wrong. My eyes shifted through the shadows. No noises emanated from within the building. Carefully, I called out "Eric?" When there was no reply, my throat constricted and I called his name again, "Eric!" The only answer I received was more silence. Something was wrong. The scales, I knew what they were, but they couldn't be. They couldn't be what I thought. It wasn't possible.

My head whipped side to side as I searched, frantically running through the building looking for Eric. The glimmering black scales littered the floor throughout the entire church, and clung to the seats on some of the chairs and tables. I rounded the corner and flung open the doors to the auditorium. Eric sat on the wooden altar, staring at the patches of colored glass as if nothing was amiss. More scattered scales lined the aisles and pews.

My voice echoed through the room before me, "Eric. What happened? Are these… " I couldn't say it. The thought. What it meant made my blood freeze in my veins.

He turned toward me, golden eyes rimmed in scarlet. The front of his shirt was torn, hanging off his body with bloody gashes across his chest. "Yes. They got out. They came looking for you… The demons are here, Ivy."

My feet crunched over the black scales until I threw myself into Eric's arms, surprising myself and him. I pulled him to me, holding him tightly. The warmth of his body reassured me that he was all right. When I pushed him away, the red ring around his irises faded. His forearms were lined with pink welts from lacerations that had started to heal. Eric tilted his head as his brow pinched. I had hugged him. The gesture confused him. That was fine, it confused me, too. I stepped away from him, eager to ignore what I just did.

"How'd they get here? Are the gates of the Underworld really open? That's the only way they can get out, right?" My eyes darted around the room. There wasn't a section of the carpet that wasn't covered in demon scales. Eric seemed sedate. His gaze remained affixed to the floor, occasionally glancing at my face. "What did you do to them?"

He stared at my face, and arched an eyebrow. "Do you really want to know?" I shook my head. I didn't want to know. I didn't want to know how many demons there were or exactly how they died. It was apparent that he skinned them somehow. I gagged back the stomach acid that climbed up my throat. I didn't need details.

Eric slid off the altar, looking down at me still somewhat baffled. I looked away, my eyes searching for more carnage, more signs of a fight. But there was nothing else. He said, "That's all that remains of that pack. There were more than I could handle. So I... did that to them. It was the only way to survive." He glanced at me. "They want you. They came here looking for you." Eric moved his arms over his chest, as he pushed his toe through a pile of shining black scales. "Do you believe me now? Do you believe he's after you?"

"No, this wasn't Collin," I replied staring at the room. My ribs were ready to splinter into a million pieces, as my heart raced in my chest. An eerie calmness protruded from my thoughts. "This was Kreturus. He's done waiting. We're out of time." Eric was standing in front of me. My gaze shot up to his face. His lips were pressed tightly together in a thin line. "The Guardian must be dead."

"Why would the Guardian be dead?" Eric shook his head, his eyes coming back to life as I spoke.

"Apryl said—something happened. She was attacked. I found her wandering through the Underworld alone. She couldn't remember what happened. They did something to her. But she thought they did something to the Guardian, as well." I turned to Eric. "If the Guardian's dead, then what's holding the demons in Hell?"

"Absolutely nothing. And there's more than demons down there that will come racing out." His arms unfolded, as he walked toward me. "We need to find Satan's Stone now. We need the last memory. Let me take it before it's too late." His hands slid around my waist as he pulled me closer without waiting for me to answer. The look on his face, the depth of the sorrow in his eyes was different. I didn't have time to consider it, or even agree to his demands. His lips were pressed to mine and he was kissing me.

As the kiss deepened, I tried to think about the things I'd learned about Satan's Stone. But it didn't seem to help. Eric's kiss didn't lighten and end as quickly it usually did. Instead, he pulled me closer, causing my waist to bend as our bodies pressed together. I could feel the heat of his skin as he pressed himself to me. His fingers tangled in my hair, pulling me nearer, tighter, as his tongue stroked mine. A chill ran down my spine. It felt like we were being watched. Breathless, I pushed him away. My fingers brushed the taste of him off my lips as I breathed through my mouth, looking up at Eric.

"Did you get it?" I asked.

He shook his head, but as Eric started to speak, another voice rang out. "So, this is what you do when I'm not around?" Collin. Collin stood there at the end of the rows of pews. Demon scales were everywhere, but he didn't seem to notice them. He glared at me. Me in Eric's arms. Me wiping away Eric's kiss from my lips.

Eric tensed at the sound of Collin's voice, and slid his arm around my waist. He jerked me back toward him tightly. His heart pounded in his chest. Eric's muscles tensed, as he spoke, "She's mine now, Smith. Leave before I make you."

Collin stepped towards me, and with every footfall my heart jumped up my throat another lurch. I didn't pull out of Eric's grip. It felt like time had frozen and thawed, and the only thing I could look at was Collin's eyes dripping with anger and envy.

Collin laughed. The sound made me skin crawl. "You think so?"

Eric's grip around my waist was crushing me, but he didn't release me. If anything he pulled me tighter. He whispered in my ear, "He seems *off*... "

And he did. Collin's body was tense, rigidly lined with tight muscles that were exuding power. The air seemed to take on a different life as he passed through. The most unnerving part wasn't that the air hissed as he neared us, it wasn't that the demon scales burned into oblivion under his feet—it was his eyes.

Ruthless, dead, wax blue eyes that fixated on my throat.

"Leave," Eric hissed in my ear. His arm loosened around my waist as he started to shove me behind him. "I'll give you a head start." I began to protest, but he only shoved me harder, "Go!"

Collin's eyes were two pools of burning fire. The slant to his shoulders, the step of his foot—none of it seemed like him. I'd seen Collin fight. I knew him, but this boy, this thing walking towards us... I didn't know at all.

I ran. Turning on my heel, I ran out the preacher's entrance and up the back stairs of the church. My feet slid across the floor as I tried to get traction and failed.

Demon scales were everywhere. What did Eric do? I didn't have time to think about it. There was no time. The black glass appeared in front of me, as I called it, and I dove through head-first.

CHAPTER THIRTY

Lying on my side, I looked up at her. Locoicia's eyes narrowed as her face pinched together. "Ivy."

Breathless, I explained, "We're out of time. Kreturus sent demons after me. They entered an old church looking for me."

The Demon Princess nodded. "So. You want your final lesson?" I nodded. Breathing hard, my chest filled with air and felt like a vice was squeezing me when I exhaled. Locoicia stood in front of me. Her dark hood hid her face. "It's simple. You call him, and say the last five spells I taught you in order."

"I thought he couldn't be summoned?" I asked, but she laughed.

"Don't be a fool. Of course you can call him. There is always one way to summon a demon, and they have no choice but to answer." The smile faded from her red lips, "But you have to be ready to slay him when you call, or you will die. Calling him is your advantage. Certainly, even Kreturus thinks he's safe. It's the one thing that I never got to use on him... " she placed her palms together and turned from me. Her long black cloak billowed as she walked.

"There are already demons attacking. Tell me how to call him! I have to end this!" the facts were pressing into my mind. Demons. Demons had broken through the gates of Hell. They were free, roaming through the world while I was here—safe inside a piece of glass where time stood still.

Turning sharply, she said, "You cannot end this, little one. It has already begun. And while you stand here in front of me, time rages on." My eyes widened in horror. Locoicia said time passed differently in the mirror. In the past, I stumbled out of the glass at approximately the same time I entered. She looked into my mortified face lost inside her black hood, perfectly calm. She lifted her fingers to my shoulder and removed a piece of lint that didn't exist. Her lips twisted into a thin smile. "There are too many things pulling on you—too many chances for you to back out of our bargain. I had to ensure that you would complete your end of the bargain. I allowed time to continue as it normally does from this side of the glass.

"Your home is now the epicenter of the battle. The gateway to the Underworld that hinges open, unguarded, is by your childhood home. All the people you grew up with, all the people you saw every day for seventeen years are in danger, as we speak. There is only one way to keep the battle from spreading. There is only one way to stop it, Ivy. You know what it is. You know what you must do. Complete the incantation, and when you do, take his power through a kiss, and use it as you will. Stop the destruction. Save what remains of your home." She gestured, sounding completely apathetic. Denial coursed through me. There was no way I could accept her words. Locoicia finally said, "Kill Kreturus. Save what you can."

"I could call them back," I said. "I could push the demons back into Hell."

She smirked at my naivety, turning from me. "Kill him, first. Then, deal with everything else." She moved across the room, and sat at the stone chair at the head of the table. Her back was straight, rigid. Her cloak masked her face, and violet eyes peered at me.

Dread grabbed a hold of my throat and squeezed. I repeated her words, "With everything else?" She nodded. I blanched, "What else is there?"

She stood in a swift, fluid motion. Her voice was louder this time, "We are wasting time. Deal with it later." She swirled toward me. The black fabric billowed at her ankles as she walked back towards me. "Your lesson. Listen carefully. Failing to do exactly as I say will have hideous consequences that you do not want to pay. Do you understand?" I nodded. I understood. The pain price would go askew and anything could happen. She nodded, tilting her head. There was excitement in her voice, a quality that was normally absent. "Calling him is simple. Conjure my glass, and then cut your left palm with a brimstone blade. Cut from," she took my palm in her leather-clad hand, and slid her finger from left to right, running across the many lines of my palm, "here to here. Wipe the blood across the black mirror and with your right hand, right to left. Then smear his name, letter by letter, into your blood with your index finger." She dropped my hand.

Her lips pulled into a tight smile as she spoke. "Within seconds, the demon will be forced through the glass. He will fall at your feet, unaware that there was any magic that could have done that to him. You must say each incantation—one per second—to kill him. You must not hesitate. The spells must be said in order, without pause. One word per second. No quicker. No slower. Begin the moment he falls through the mirror. After the fifth word falls from your lips, the demon king will die at your feet. And when he dies, perform your demon kiss on him, but instead of taking his soul, you will be stealing his power." She pressed her fingertips together, as she paused. Her voice became lighter, more amused. "And you will be the Demon Queen."

A chill ran down my spine, but I didn't shudder. Nothing moved me. I nodded and turned away from her. I placed my hand on the glass, and felt it melt beneath my palm. Looking over my shoulder, I asked, "And you have taught me everything? Everything I need to know to defeat Kreturus?"

Her lips twisted into a confident smile. "Yes. My end of the bargain is complete. Go kill your demon, little one. I'll call for you when it's time to complete your end of the deal, and bring me my angel." With that, I slipped through the mirror and stepped back into the church.

CHAPTER THRITY-ONE

Silence screamed through the darkness. Not a sound came from the place I'd left Eric and Collin. My chest swelled as I drew a breath. I didn't dare call out. Instead, I moved slowly, quietly, one foot at a time. Splintered wood lent to the rubble strewn beneath my feet. There wasn't a single pew remaining. They had all been smashed to splinters. The rainbow of colored glass that hung in the rose window was laying scattered across the floor. The blood red pieces of glass gleamed like pools of blood amidst the rubble.

I didn't see Eric or Collin. Neither was dead on the floor. They were both gone. I walked to the end of the row, and crouched to move through the doors that were blasted off their hinges. And the sight on the other side stripped every sense of right and wrong from my body. Suddenly there was no meaning to anything. Shock sucked the breath from my body in one swift motion as I gazed in disbelief. For a second I didn't realize I'd stopped breathing until I sucked a gasp of air. I was outside and the front of the church was gone— ripped off and hoisted away. Rubble scattered across the remains of the front lawn that was now pitted with holes and dirty snow. The winter wind bit my cheeks and tossed my hair wildly about, as I gazed in horror.

Destruction was as far as I could see. Locoicia's words meant nothing to me until I saw it with my own eyes. The church, the little brown ugly church that had stood in the center of a nice little neighborhood, was gone. The houses were gone. The streets were torn to shreds. Asphalt was cracked into pebbles that scattered through the snow. Wind bit into my cheeks as it whipped by, unaware of the things happening— unaware of the horror that stole my breath. The only thing that remained was the center of the church building where I'd emerged. The beautiful houses that lined the street stood in piles of burning rubble. Streams of smoke littered the landscape with various size plumes reaching upward. The sky was a color I'd never seen before. The entire thing was streaked in shades of scarlet. It was as if God himself were bleeding into the heavens and staining the sky.

As far as I could see, everything was the same; broken homes, shattered glass, splintered, burning wood under a bleeding sky. Plumes of smoke choked the snow out of the air. My feet faltered, as I staggered back, not believing what my eyes saw. Blackened bodies, twisted into deformed shapes of gleaming black scales and burning red eyes moved in the distance. Demons. They moved between the smoke and rubble walking farther and farther away from me. They marched onward to destroy the homes and families that lay beyond the horizon. There was no formation as they moved. It was strange. The demons were clearly moving as a unit, but it didn't look like any formation I'd ever seen. Someone was commanding them.

I turned slowly, almost too afraid to look behind me, when I saw him standing a few yards away. "Eric." I breathed his name as if it were my last breath. His hands were at his sides, covered in blood and black soot. His shirt clung onto his chest by a few threads. His brimstone blade was in his hand. He watched me with uncertain eyes. I ran to him, stopping a short distance away. "Eric," I breathed again. "Eric, what happened?"

He glared at me. Hatred wasn't hidden in his eyes; it was front and center, burning like wild fire. He reached for my throat, crunching my collarbone under his hands. I didn't scream, as I heard the bone crack in his grip. The pain registered somewhere in the back of my mind. I slipped out of his hold and remained far enough away so he couldn't grab me again. The bone began to mend itself.

Eric's face was covered in sweat despite the snow. He breathed, flaring his nostrils, his shoulders tensed and his arms ready to fight. "You," he spat. "You did this. Where have you been?" he yelled. "I held him off and you disappeared."

My eyes flicked to the destroyed landscape and back to Eric's face, "I wasn't gone that long, and… "

He rushed at me, and I was too shocked to move. Eric grabbed my wrists, and pulled them up to my neck, pinning them together. His body shook as he stared at me, increasing the pressure on my wrists. "And, nothing. You left. And now you come back? Now you want to save us?" He laughed, and threw me to the side. My body landed hard on the frozen ground forcing the air out of my lungs. I gasped, looking up as Eric began to walk away into the burning sun that was setting in front of him.

I shot up, and he turned with speed that I didn't expect. "I had no choice. How much time has passed?"

There wasn't a speck of gold in his eyes, "Five weeks. It's been five weeks since you left me here. Five weeks of hiding, of running, of fighting. There's nothing left. The demons destroyed everything looking for you." His gaze raked my body, and he laughed. "And I thought... "

"You thought what?" my voice scratched from inhaling so much smoke. The wind shifted and we were lost inside a cloud of burning rubble. I coughed, unable to see him. "I was gone for seconds, seconds! When I came back, you were gone! There was nothing left." I paused. "I thought you found the memory you needed. I thought that you... "

His fingers wrapped around my arm, digging into my skin. Eric pressed his face to mine, "You thought what?" he hissed through the smoke. "You thought I found what I needed? You thought I found where the Satan's Stone is?" He shook me hard, yanking me out of the cloud of smoke as he did it. "There was nothing. Nothing. None of that memory remained in your mind. I searched for it, but it was gone." The cloud of smoke was behind us, as Eric pressed his face to mine, spitting words in rapid succession.

Something inside me stirred, dropping into my stomach like lead. "So the book... The page... " I asked, looking into his face. "It was for nothing? You don't know where the stone is?"

His grip dug in tighter before he released me. "Where were you? Where did you go while your world bled to death? Every Valefar was forced to slay anything that breathed, while they searched for you. Collin was in the first wave to show up. Since then there has been nothing but attacks. Your screwed up blood spared me from being forced to battle with the Valefar. I have their mark on my face, but I killed them just the same. I waited for you. Hoping you'd come back. But you didn't. Where were you? " His voice was rough. Eric's gaze searched over my shoulder before returning to my face.

I couldn't tell him. The blood bargain forbade me to speak of it. It prevented the words from tumbling out of my mouth. So I did the next best thing and I called the demon glass. Eric turned his head looking at the place next to me as it shimmered and turned black. Within moments the Glass of Locoicia stood next to me. I pointed to it, "I was in there. My blood bargain required me to go. Time usually stops when I step inside, but this time, it didn't."

Eric's eyes were wide. A flicker of gold swirled around his black pupils before extinguishing. He leaned towards it, and then pulled me away like it was poison. "Shit. Is that what I think it is? How do you find this shit? Fuck Ivy!" He ripped his hands through his hair and looked down at me. "Your blood bargain was with

Locoicia? She did this?" I nodded, watching rage and fear collide in his eyes.

"She knew I couldn't stop this, either that or she made certain that I couldn't stop this." Turning my head, I gazed at the landscape. There was no trace of suburbia. It looked like someone dropped acid on the ground and smashed the trees with boulders. The ground was cracked and covered in rubble and blood. Glittering black scales floated by on the breeze. Plumes of smoke rose into the air from a million places of differing size. This was the epicenter of the destruction. Maybe I couldn't stop it. It was too late for that, but maybe I could do something else. If I was their Queen, they would have no choice. I turned to Eric. "I have to call him. I have to end this. Or there will be nothing left." The bleak landscape said there was already nothing left, but I couldn't accept it.

He shook his head, "I don't know where the stone is. Without it, you're too weak."

Ignoring him, I grabbed the black blade out of his hand. Eric watched with his lips parted, as I pushed the blade against my palm. A thin red line trailed after the blade as it swept across my palm. When I finished, I thrust the blade back into his grip. Stepping toward the mirror, I raised my arm. Streamers of blood ran down my wrist and dripped on the earth at my feet. I pressed my fingers to the glass, feeling its sudden resistance beneath my palm. Swallowing hard, I wiped my bloody hand across the black glass.

"Ivy," Eric said from behind me, "Don't. Don't do this. Assuming Illeca is alive and she told you this, you… You just can't trust her."

Silence filled the air. I stared at the mirror watching my blood change the nature of the glass. Our reflections appeared within its smoky depths. I knew Eric was right, but it was too late for that. It was go forward and kill Kreturus or die. "I made a blood bargain, Eric." I glanced at him as I lifted my right pointer finger and smeared K onto the glass. "She can't lie."

He grabbed my shoulder and twisted me around, "What are you, new? Of course she can lie! She'll break the bargain in a heartbeat if she thinks it'll free her. And you're too weak to do a damn thing about it. Shit! We should have found the stone when we had the chance!" He turned from me, and I stopped halfway through smearing the letter R. "I feel like I should know. I can feel it, but I can't remember. Why do I know about it? Why did I know about Satan's Stone at all?"

My eyes slid over his body. He was sincerely asking. My face went slack as the answer came to me. I suddenly knew why he knew about the stone. Why he had notes in his book. Why he was the authoritative expert on the subject. Eric saw it happen, he saw the curve of my mouth drop, and the recognition in my eyes as my hand moved away from the glass in shock. Eric yanked me away from the mirror.

He flung me to the ground, pouncing like a crazed cat, and pinned my shoulders to the frozen earth. "Tell me. You know. I saw it in your eyes. You know something."

CHAPTER THIRTY-TWO

Eric shook my shoulders, but I called shadows. Within seconds they snaked down my throat and protruded from me until they wrapped around his arms, and pulled him off of me. I rose, and walked back to the glass and added the letter E. My blood didn't dry or freeze or drip down the black mirror. The swipe of blood was exactly as I'd left it.

Eric cursed me over my shoulder, screaming obscenities at my back. I shook my head, considering the explanation. "It can't be. It makes no sense. You had a life, a wife—and Al found you." I smeared the letter T. "I was mistaken." I turned to look back at him.

Eric was held to the ground with invisible bonds as shadows snaked around his wrists and feet, binding him to the earth. I turned back to the glass and smeared an U through the blood before Eric spoke.

"Don't make me do it," he said. I turned to look at him after I wrote R on the glass. "I'll kill you the same way I killed those demons the last time I saw you. Their skin was filleted from their bodies. That's why there were scales everywhere. And that was only the beginning... And don't think I can't do it. It has nothing to do with how powerful I am. Don't think it won't have any effect on you, cause it will. It's your power, not mine. When I kissed you searching for the memories, I borrowed some of your power. Only the tiniest drop, small enough that you didn't notice." But I did notice. I'd felt the power drain, but didn't realize what he did. It wasn't the venom that weakened me after Eric's kiss, it was Eric! His fists clenched into balls at his sides, as he writhed on the ground fighting against the shadows that bound him. Smoke billowed around us, blowing in the winter wind. Eric growled, "Don't make me do it, Ivy. I will. If you write one more letter on the glass without releasing me, you'll force my hand. I can't sit here, tied up and let you do this. If she lied to you, you could free Locoicia, and then we'll have to deal with her and Kreturus."

Watching him squirm at my feet, I said nothing. I blinked once, making my decision. My arms folded across my chest. There was a moment. I could pause now, but once the last letter was strewn across the mirror, I could not stop. The shadows fled from Eric as soon as I released them. He sucked in a jagged breath before jumping to his feet. His gaze burned into my body as he walked toward me, but I didn't blink or back away. "Explain it." I was certain that her lie would be detectable. "How do you summon a demon?"

Eric looked at the glass, and then back at me, "He'll effonate to you, using your power to do so, when you call his name, but… "

"And if the demon is bound? Then how do you call him?" I asked glaring at him.

"There is no way to call a bound demon. The magic used to hold him will prevent you from effonating him." Eric pointed at the mirror, shaking his head. "You see. Something's wrong. This shouldn't be here. This blood and glass should have nothing to do with calling a demon." He looked at the reflectionless glass. "What's it supposed to do?"

I was wasting time. The world around me was dying. Curtly, I replied, "My blood, a brimstone blade, and his name is supposed to suck Kreturus through this glass. The moment he is through, I'll kill him. Eric. It's our only chance. It won't exhaust my power. It'll end this. Isn't that what you want?"

More gold flickered through his eyes like a light bulb that was about to burn out. He drank in my face like he'd never see me again. Eric pressed his lips together and stepped away from the glass, sweeping his arm forward, allowing me to write the last two letters on the glass.

Staring at Eric from the corner of my eye, I stepped passed him. My blood clung to the glass with all but two letters to complete his name.

I lifted my hand to the glass with my index finger outstretched. Pressing my finger against the black glass, I carefully smeared the remaining letters. My eyes shifted from the mirror to Eric. My gaze ran down his tense shoulders to the black blade that was clenched in his grip. He was half crouched, and ready to fight whatever came through the glass.

My blood-strewn letters soaked into the glass. It was like watching letters cast in magic marker disperse in water. Our reflections appeared in the glass. It was changing. I could see Eric standing behind me, watching the enchanted mirror, and waiting... The black pane came to life. It rippled once, then twice. I reached for my hair, grabbing my comb. The tines extended, as I pressed them to my mark. Demon magic flowed through my veins as I called to it. Anticipation and determination cemented inside of me, as I felt Eric step closer.

The words of the dark magic Illeca had trained me to say lingered on the tip of my tongue. A dark form appeared in the glass, as if it were very far away. A figure stood frozen, getting pushed towards us at incredible speed. Good. It was working. I tasted the words in my mouth, rolling the death spell over my tongue. My heart raced inside of my head, as I watched the figure get closer and closer. What took a matter of seconds seemed to last a lifetime. Kreturus stood with his head slumped, appearing completely human. My jaw tightened at the sight. Locoicia said it would be easier to kill him in human form. A tangle of dark hair masked his downturned face as the glass forced him forward. Faster and faster he approached, and the words were ready, ready to say—ready to kill.

My mind was disconnected from my emotions, as it needed to be. Dread didn't wash over me in cold sheets. I stood there facing the being that would kill me, and felt no fear. But in the back of my mind, something whispered—something I promptly suppressed.

The figure in the glass didn't slow. He was hurdling faster, frozen, unmoving as he was summoned to die by my hand. I stared with hatred at the broad shoulders, and the dark hair that covered his face. His body hurled through the glass as if he were no heavier than a piece of lint. I didn't have time to think, and by the time his body pressed to the glass, it was too late. The words were ready to roll off my tongue. They had to. There was no alternative. No choice. And it was more than my bargain with the Demon Princess that forced me to say the spells. I had to stop the destruction that was strewn around me. And the only way to stop the demons was to kill the one commanding them. There was no going backwards. There was no other way.

CHAPTER THIRTY-THREE

I uttered the first word as the boy was thrown through the glass, and cast face-down on the ground at my feet. He shook his head and curved his shoulders to rise, but the spell grabbed hold of him. He tried to free himself as the spell threw him down. His voice was gravelly—unearthly—like a voice suspended in a throat-tearing scream. A second passed. No more, no less.

The next word fell from my lips and splashed to the ground. His head turned to the side. Dark hair covered his face, as the spell crushed the breath out of his lungs, pinning him to the ground. His body heaved, making the sounds of a drowning man gasping for his breath. One second passed. No emotion filled me. I didn't care that he couldn't breathe. I didn't care that it was my words that were killing him. I felt nothing. No compulsion to stop, no empathy—nothing.

My mouth opened and the third word fell forth. His gravelly voice, a voice that was trying to speak to me, was suddenly muted. Though his mouth moved, not sound protruded. I caught a glimpse of Eric's face in the mirror. His eyes burned with hatred, but his gaze seemed shocked.

Another second.

Another word.

Another spell.

There was no mercy. I uttered a fourth word. The boy's back arched, but his body was still pinned to the ground. His mouth open in a silent scream. I could see every tooth inside his mouth. The veins in his neck were ready to pop, as his eyes were crushed together trying to endure the pain I inflicted.

One word left. Only one word remained.

As I watched, waiting for the second to pass, something whispered at the back of mind. This was not what I expected Kreturus to look like. He was vulnerable in this form. Why would he use it? Was he really just the victim of faulty timing? Was it true that luck was with me, and I caught him in a human body, instead of his own hideous form? I watched the boy as his pale pink lips remained parted in agony, frozen in a silent scream that never ended.

The pain price was about to slam into me. Payment would be made as the fifth word rolled off my tongue. The spell was death. After I said the word, the boy's writhing would stop. His body would go limp at my feet in less than a second. Hideous things would happen to me for uttering the words I said. The pain price would be unbearable. I stared at the boy. Kreturus had already killed him. At best he was a Valefar. Death would free this boy, and let him die in peace, while the rest of us figured out how to endure the new Hell.

One word left. The second swept by, surreally slow. The boy's face remained contorted in pain and covered by his dark hair. As I moved my jaw, and slid my lips around the final word, a plume of smoke blew into my face. I pressed my eyes closed and heard my voice ringing the beginning of the death incantation in my ears. The wind whipped the smoke away quickly. My gaze fell down to the boy screaming in agony at my feet. The sudden gust revealed his face. And I saw him.

Collin.

I felt nothing. Shock didn't wash over me. Horror didn't twist my stomach into a thousand tiny knots. My voice didn't ring forth, ripping out of my throat with complete devastation. I felt nothing as I saw his beautiful face contorted in pain. His eyes were pressed closed, trapped in a silent scream. His face. His perfect face was in utter agony. Collin's normally smooth and confident brow was wrinkled in torment. His lips, the lips he'd pressed to mine—the perfectly pale pink lips that I wanted to cover my body—they were pulled back in silent horror. His screams didn't resonate. He writhed at my feet, bound on the frozen earth.

The word, the last incantation was pouring from my lips, unable to stop. The words were already falling from my mouth when I saw his face. I couldn't stop. I couldn't withdraw the words. I stared at him with horror screaming through my mind like a rush of wind that I couldn't feel. There was no choice. Tears did not stream down my face. Numbness flowed through me as I looked down at Collin, knowing that his death was imminent.

Silence followed the final word. A black shimmer surrounded his body and dissipated. If I blinked, I wouldn't have noticed. Part of me wondered if that was the last bit of his soul leaving his body. Eric stood behind me, wide eyed, and staring. That was when the pain price began. It was designed to start after the last word was spoken. It was made so that I could say all five spells in succession without pause. Without hesitation. Without error. The price of all five spells began, one after the other.

I stood perfectly still, staring straight ahead. My jaw locked as the first wave of agony washed over me. Breath was choked from my body as every piece of muscle was shredded to bits within me. The muscles that were normally woven together, unwrapped strand by strand. Pain coursed through me. It was only in my mind. It wasn't really happening. That was the way it worked last time, but this time I wasn't so sure. My mind didn't connect with the pain, although I felt my body screaming inside my head.

I didn't move. I didn't flinch. I felt nothing. Sucking in a breath of air, the next pain price started. My fist balled at my side. I stared as Eric moved to face me, utterly fascinated. His eyes slid over my body in a way that was too sensual. When his gaze touched my throat, it felt as if it was split opened with a hot knife, and wrenched back. The muscles in my neck tensed. My control was faltering. The price of these spells was higher than I expected.

The next two payments in pain doubled up. My mind was screaming, telling me to stop it or I'd die, but I couldn't stop this. There was no reprieve. There was no other choice but to bear the agony I cast on myself. My body stood frozen, unwilling and unable to move. I was aware of Eric, but my gaze fixated on Collin. He lay motionless where he fell. His dark hair rustled as the wind whipped it about. His fingers didn't twitch. His chest didn't rise or fall.

The final pain price crashed into me, and I fell to the ground. Blood poured from my mouth, soaking the earth under my face. The pain price was real this time. It wasn't only in my mind. The pain tore through me, spilling my blood as it went. The pain price of death was blood. The price rebounded and doubled as it tore through me, intensifying. My body stiffened in response, trying to deal with the agony. The venom in my chest burned, suddenly brought to life. My fingers wanted to move and clutch my chest, but I couldn't. Weakness held my head to the frozen dirt. The chill didn't pierce my skin. I felt nothing. I did not move. My eyes were the only part of me that retained motion. Eric's foot was next to my head, as he watched me at his feet. I couldn't see his face.

As the pain raked through me, more blood spilled from my lips. The warm liquid spilled over my lips, pooling under my cheek. The poison burned in my chest. It was moving. Flowing. I could sense it within me. My gaze fixated on Collin's face as the pain price began to fade. Every inch of me was numb. There was no comfort. There was no one to help me pick up the pieces when I rose. There was nothing left of my previous life. Warm blood had collected under my head, sticking to the side of my face and seeping into my hair. My lips were parted, and a trail of crimson streaked along my cheek and to the ground.

I stared at his lifeless face, not thinking anything. Not feeling anything. I knew I should be horrified. I knew emotions should be crashing violently through my body, but there was nothing. Only silence. When my fists opened, Eric leaned down next to me. I didn't move. I couldn't speak.

"Take his power. Finish this before she comes." Eric was looking at the glass still expecting Locoicia to come forth, but I knew she wouldn't. "She needed someone to pay the pain price that she couldn't. Hurry." His hand was on my shoulder, his grip under my arms, pulling me up onto his lap. His fingers pressed into my cheeks as he tried to move my lifeless body. "You don't die today, do you hear me?" My lashes slowly lowered and reopened. Eric's face was overflowing with emotion. He felt everything. I felt nothing. We were so fucked up. "Kiss him, Ivy. Take your power and heal yourself. I can't mend these wounds. You have to."

He pushed me forward, as if I could walk. But, my body protested and wouldn't support my weight. I slumped to the ground. My arms moved quick enough to break my fall, but they were too weak to hold me up. The muscles trembled, and my arms bent suddenly launching me face-first into the ground. Dirt scratched into the blood and stuck to my skin.

Eric sighed and his arms were gripping me again, pulling me toward Collin's body. "I'd take his power myself, if I could, but only the one who killed him can claim it—and we sure as hell want it. Locoicia will come, Ivy. There is no way she won't. And right now, she's powerful enough to kill us both. I used the power I stole from you. You have to do this." He dragged me toward Collin as he spoke. My throat tightened and I didn't think I was breathing anymore. My eyelids wanted to close. They felt so heavy. Eric's hand met my cheek in a hard swipe. "Wake up," he said as he dropped me next to Collin's body. "Finish this."

CHAPTER THIRTY-FOUR

There was no power left within me. The venom was snaking through my veins making me weaker by moment. My arm felt like lead, but I lifted it, turning Collin's face toward me. His body was still warm. Lifeless. I couldn't believe he was Kreturus. It didn't make sense. I didn't understand. Eric's foot was on my back, pushing me on top of Collin's chest. I pressed my hand to Collin's cheek, waiting to feel something. Remorse. Anger. Something. But there was emotion. No bond. Only Eric's shoe in my back. I pressed my forehead to his lips, and looked at his face one last time. I didn't want the power within him. I would have died there, laying on top of him. But I heard them. The sounds grew louder and louder. Screams. People. The demons were returning for their master, and I'd killed him. There would be a power vacuum if I didn't take it. I had to. There was no choice.

I lowered my face, and pressed my lips to his. The stirring sensation that craved Collin came awake within me. As it slid down his throat, eyes of ice and fire flicked opened. Collin sucked in a ragged breath, throwing me off of him. He clawed at the dirt behind him, moving away from me. He glared at me with utter hatred. Eric's hand was on my shoulder, trying to pull me to my feet. I stared, unable to shut my mouth— utterly shocked.

He was alive.

The spell didn't work.

The emotions that were held back suddenly came to me in a rush. My heart shattered into a million pieces. Every breath felt like a knife in my gut. I wanted to scream. I wanted to claw his face off with my bare hands, but I remained silent... Perfectly still, staring at him. My voice was a rush of air. It was barely audible, but he heard me, "You're Kreturus."

A weak smile snaked across his lips as the pressure on my shoulder from Eric increased. Eric was trying to pull me away, but my feet wouldn't move. I didn't turn. For some reason, my shoulders shook him off as I stepped toward the liar. The deceiver. I couldn't stop looking into his eyes. Collin said nothing. There was a voice screaming inside my mind, so blaringly loud that I couldn't stand it for another second. I repressed the emotions the feelings that were telling me that I would die. I could barely hear my words, "You used me."

He leaned in close to my face. Close enough to touch me. I tensed, ready to attack. Collin lifted his hands, palms up showing me he wouldn't come closer. "I didn't mean to—I… didn't want to. I'm not Kreturus. Not right now. But when you pulled me through the mirror," he looked back at, "we were the same person. What Kreturus does isn't like possession. It's more horrifying. It's like we fuse. I'm subject to his whims, but I can still think, act, and feel. Your spell tore us apart. And since he can't be up here without me, I assume he was sucked back down into Hell. But there's no way to know for certain. I don't know what other effects your incantation had. It didn't work the way it should have, and I think we both know why." He paused for a moment, watching me. There could only be one reason why Collin was still alive. Something altered the spell. Something protected him. Something powerful. His fingers flexed once and then straightened at his sides, "The last time I saw you he was with me, making me tear everything apart to find you. He thinks you'll submit to him. He thinks you'll willingly be his queen."

I stared at him, not believing a word he said. My eyes slid over his face. The bond was destroyed. There was no way to know if he was lying. "You're two different beings? But sometimes you're not?" I didn't believe him. He could hear it in my voice.

Collin swallowed, "It's difficult to explain. When I was younger—a new Valefar—I wanted my soul back. I was rash. I didn't think. I thought I'd win... " He searched my face, but no emotions swam across it. His eyes shifted away from mine, ashamed, "I found Kreturus and made a blood bargain. It can't be broken. He got use of me and my body to find the Prophecy One and free him from his prison. In exchange, when he finally had you—I'd get my soul back. But the bargain didn't go the way I thought... And I didn't know it would be you." He pressed his lips together, waiting for me to speak, but I remained silent. "Ivy, when I realized you were the one I was supposed to hand over—I couldn't do it. I defaulted. I lost. He's been using me to lure you to him. He wants you and will do anything to have you."

Collin's voice was pleading, begging me to understand, "I didn't want this. I didn't want the prophecy. I did everything I could think of to derail it, and prevent it from happening. But it didn't matter what I did. Prophecies happen." He looked down at me, pushing the hair out of his eyes as he looked to the ground, "I wanted to warn you, but I couldn't tell you about the bargain. But, just now, something changed when you cast your spell, and the magic that was gagging me from speaking—it faded. I still can't tell you everything, but I can acknowledge what's already happened. Ivy, I can't control him. Kreturus is part of me, and has no reason to release me. The things around you—the death and destruction—it was all by my hands."

I was silent. His words swam in my mind like distant islands that I couldn't reach. The words tumbled out of my mouth with a chilled sharpness to them that I didn't hear when I thought it in my mind. "Did you love me at all? Or was that Kreturus playing me?"

The corner of his lips pulled into a sad smile. Collin pushed his hands into his pockets and hung his head. "It hardly matters now. But…" blue eyes pierced me as he looked up, locking his eyes with mine, "I've dreamt of being with you, falling asleep in your arms. It's your lips I wanted on my body. It's your hands I wanted tangled in my hair. It's your voice I wanted to hear speak my name in ecstasy… " His eyes burned as they slid over me.

Collin reached for me. I didn't move. My body felt like it was made of stone, cold and unfeeling. His hand slipped around my neck, as he pushed back my hair. He whispered to me as his warm breath moved across my lips, "I love you. I always have. I always will."

A million pieces of me screamed from within, wanting to fall to the cold ground and fade from existence. I was so numb that his caress meant nothing. His words meant nothing. There was no response, no relief, no regret. Nothing. Nothing as his sapphire eyes gazed at me and his fingers swirled around a curl at the nape of my neck. I swallowed. My mouth felt like it was full of sand. "That's why the prophecy says you die— because Kreturus is killed. And you are with him when it happens."

Collin nodded. "I wish I could change it. I wish…" but he never got to say it. The sky above him began to move, swirling like ink and blood. Kreturus was coming.

"I still want you. I can't let him take you again," Eric's grip nearly slid off my shoulder, but I grabbed it with my hand. I started the effonation the moment the sky changed. It had started within me already, and I shrouded it with shadows so no one would feel its heat. Not Eric. And not Collin. It was draining every last bit of power I had left.

The smile on Collin's face faded, making something deep within me stir. Collin said, "The bargain I made killed me. Never think it was you…"

Collin's spine stiffened as he looked up. "You need to go. Go before he calls me back, or worse."

I nodded once. Then, the flames shot through my stomach and the shadows slipped away, revealing the coursing heat that enveloped us. Eric's grip on me tightened as I pulled him away with me. The night was swallowed up around us in tongues of flames as the Demon King returned to Collin.

CHAPTER THIRTY-FIVE

We landed hard on the floor of the Lorren. I screamed, clutching my chest as the poison burned within. Eric got to his knees and leaned over me. A hand reached down and pulled him away, and then swept under me. I managed to utter, "Don't kill him," to Eric before I passed out.

Voices penetrated my ears before I slid my eyes open. Eric was speaking, "She won't do it. It doesn't matter."

Lorren answered, annoyed, "You can't expect me to believe that she'll kill him when the time comes if she didn't do it already."

"You can't expect anything from her… " Eric retorted.

"I said the spell," I answered sitting up. The poison was still in my chest. I could feel it. A metallic blue flower twisted between Lorren's fingers. He drew out more of the venom, pulling it away from my heart. My weakness had faded with sleep. I was shocked that neither one of them killed me. Their heads turned in my direction. "I meant to kill him, but something went wrong. It was like the last word only stunned him. And split him from Kreturus. I didn't default on my end of the bargain. The spell didn't work." I punched the solid gold bench I was laying on and it dented beneath my fist with a loud thud.

Eric asked, "He said you knew why it didn't work."

I glared at him, "I didn't know if that was the reason or not. And it wasn't a good time to discuss it…"

"But," Lorren said, "if you have even the slightest idea why he survived…"

I growled my reply, "My soul. My soul was in his body. It protected him. I don't know why or how. Locoicia didn't know it was there. I never told her." Staring at both of them, I added. "But you both knew. Didn't you? You knew Kreturus was still in Collin. What I saw in the Underworld wasn't a hoax. For a while, I thought it was smoke and mirrors—but it wasn't. You knew that the demon was using Collin to get to me. You knew they fused into the same person." I stood walking over to Eric. "How could you not tell me?"

His eyes were glistening. They were not completely gold, but lacking the fire that poured through them earlier. "I suspected, but there was no way to know for sure. Things aren't obvious. Collin hid it, but the way he acts is almost bipolar sometimes. It made me wonder why. And I doubted that they were the same person until the day you disappeared. Collin did all that. I saw it with my own eyes. Collin started this. More demons followed him into the church, looking for you. I barely held him off long enough for you to escape. Then, when I couldn't find you," Eric paused. His eyes shifted back to me. "I thought he killed you. But he didn't leave. Collin kept burning, and killing, looking for something—looking for you."

"That's why you were there? That's why you were near the church when I stepped outside?" He nodded once, and instantly averted his eyes. "And you," I said turning to Lorren. I wanted to kick him for not telling me. I wanted to cause him pain for what he did. "You. You fucking angel—stuck in hell. What'd you forget to tell me, huh?"

Lorren was still dressed in his black clothes. "I forgot nothing." He turned his back to me, refusing to say more.

I shot out of my chair, grabbed his shoulder and screamed in his face. "You were the angel who used the stone! It was you in the first war. You were the warrior who took the brunt of the curse, and you got trapped down here because of it, right?" Lorren's eyes drifted across my face, to Eric's, and back. He nodded once. "And the second angel… " Lorren's neck snapped in my direction with a warning in his eye, but I kept speaking. There'd been too many secrets. I wouldn't lend to allowing them to exist any further. "The second angel who used the stone to stop Kreturus is also here, isn't he?"

Eric's face pinched in confusion as he looked from Lorren to me. "What are you talking about?"

"Tell him," I said to Lorren. But Lorren just looked up at him with pinched eyes. "I already know. There's no point in hiding the damn stone. I'm on your side, and if you believed me the first two times I met you, this wouldn't have happened." Anger coursed through me and I grabbed onto it like a kite string about to slip away. Spinning on my heel, I swung my arm back and made my fist collide with a wall of golden flowers. I no longer cared what they were or who they were. They were dead. Like everyone else on earth would be if they kept playing games, and hiding things. "Tell him!"

Lorren's dark eyes met Eric's. He sighed, his back slumping, "Satan's Stone has two parts. They separate after they are used. One half finds the next owner, while the previous half remains with the last owner. The stone knows who it's destined to go to." Lorren looked at me, as if to ask if he had to continue. He finally looked back at Eric, and said, "Someone used the stone after me, which is why I no longer have it. Ivy has the one half of Satan's Stone hanging around her neck—it found her, the way it should have." Lorren glanced at me as if to ask if I was really sure.

I nearly bit his head off, "TELL HIM!"

Lorren bit down, and returned his gaze to Eric. Eric watched the two of us, saying nothing. Lorren finally spit it out, "The second angel who used Satan's Stone, the angel that was there when they sealed Kreturus into his tomb—was you. You were an angel, Eric. You were a Seraphim, a warrior. The cost of the stone made you mortal. The price was different for you than it was for me. I remember my past life. My wings were ripped off my back and I was hurled into the Underworld to spend the rest of my life. But, you" Lorren said gesturing to Eric, "you had a different destiny. The stone wasn't finished with you, yet. You were granted humanity, grew up, and were marked as a

Martis. Althea, swore to me she'd find you and raise you. She knew who you were, and she knew she'd die by your hand. It was the cost—the cost of the stone. So was everything that happened after. You were one of the few uncorrupt Martis, because you were an angel first. You saw right from wrong, even if they didn't. You're a Valefar now, because of… "

Eric cut him off, "Because of her." He glared at me.

But Lorren rose and stood in front of him, "No. You are alive because of her. You are a Valefar, if you can call it that, because of the cost of the stone. You were put into a perpetual state of change where you can't control the things around you. You cannot save her. You cannot save anything. You merely survive. That is your curse. That was your cost." Lorren tilted his head toward me and said, "I have no idea what her cost will be."

Eric looked crestfallen. His gaze shifted from Lorren to the floor as he pushed his hands out of his hair. "Nothing's as it seems, is it?" Lorren shook his head. Eric looked up, "So the other half of the stone is… "

"Gone," I said. "It's gone. You were the last person to have it. That's why you had all those notes, Eric. That's why you knew everything. Your previous lives were forgotten every time your mortality ended.

You were reborn with a new life—up until your last birth. You wrote everything of importance down so you wouldn't forget. How you found that book over the centuries is beyond me, but that's what you did. That's why you knew what Satan's Stone was in the first place—you were the last person to use it." I stood pacing, uncertain what to do next.

Eric spoke, "There's no other option then, is there?" I looked over at him. "I have to remember where I put the other half of the stone."

"The memories are gone, Eric." I turned to look back at Lorren. Something he said had just sank into my spinning brain, "What do you mean, he's a Valefar, if you can call him that?"

Lorren looked up at me. "Eric's not a Valefar. He's been demon kissed, and his soul was stripped away, but he's not under Kreturus' control. The rest of the Valefar are. Eric is not. He's under your control, Ivy."

I nearly choked as a laugh ripped out of my stomach. Both boys looked at me like I was nuts. "Eric's not under anyone's control." Lorren started to reply, but I cut him off, "Is Eric's soul here? Is it in the Pool of Lost Souls?"

Lorren nodded, "It should be. If you truly drank his soul, and I can sense that you did," Lorren did not hide his revulsion, "then it's in the Pool."

Eric rose, and took my hand in his. His voice was urgent, "I know what you're thinking." He gazed into my eyes. The scent of his blood hit me hard, and I pulled away. Eric turned toward Lorren, "No one can sense us here, within the Lorren, can they?"

Lorren shook his head, "No. The dead mask the living. This is the only place where they won't look for you. It's the only place you can hide, but eventually, I would expect Kreturus to figure it out.

"The Guardian is dead. All the other points that held the Underworld under the world have been breached. Demons walk in the sun. The sky bleeds, the clouds cry icy drops of blood. It only continues to worsen, unless you kill him, Ivy." Lorren's eyes met mine. He doubted me, I could see it on his face.

My jaw locked. I could blame him forever, but it wouldn't stop what was happening. It was too late to save the past. Salvaging what was left was the best we could hope for. "Everything would have happened to this point anyway, right?" I asked looking at both of them.

They nodded. Eric spoke, "This was the prophecy. This was the part that was not preventable."

"Then," I replied, "the rest is still up for grabs, and I'm not going down without a fight. The spell fazed Collin, which means my bargain with Locoicia is broken. If it was my failure, I'd be dead or locked in her throne room. But Im not. I'm standing here staring at you." Lorren glanced at Eric. They both seemed nervous. "I need to find the stone and end this. I'm not listening to any more fucking demons. Or angels." I glared at Lorren. "I'm ending this. I don't care what the cost of the stone is—I'm going to find it, and I'm going to use it. And next time I see Collin, this will end."

H.M. Ward

The 13th Prophecy
Demon Kissed #5

Coming

March 6, 2012

VALEFAR
Vol. 1

By H.M. Ward

CHAPTER ONE

369 days before Ivy is attacked on her 17th birthday.

"Legend states that there were thirteen prophecies that foretold the destruction of the Earth, the annihilation of the Martis and Valefar, and the obliteration of the demon Kreturus..." Jake paused as he always did when he spoke of this with Collin. It didn't matter how many times they'd talked about it, Collin's response was always the same.

Collin turned away from his friend with his arms folded. His dark shirt clung to his chest defining the muscles beneath. He looked side to side; making sure no one was listening. They were backstage in the school's theater. Long black drapes hung floor to ceiling in front of them and a cement wall was directly behind them.

Collin didn't like Jake speaking of this here, now, so he cut him off in a hushed whisper, "And that prophecy infers my death. I know, Jake."

Collin knew the prophecy, and he knew more about it than Jake did. However, he kept those comments to himself. The younger Valefar had proved to be trustworthy over time. Well, as much as a Valefar could be trusted. Turning to Jake he saw the worry pinched on his face and the tension that lined his arms—tension that wasn't normally present in this Valefar.

Collin's eyes turned to slits as he stepped toward his friend slowly, "What do you know." It was a command, not a question.

Jake was Collin's second in command. The hierarchy of the Valefar was precarious at best, and more accurately described as a savage blood bath. No other Valefar had ever been able to hold power as long as Collin had, and despite Jake's age, he knew it. Befriending Collin ensured his longevity. It had occurred to him to keep this information to himself, because if Collin was destroyed, then Jake could take his place. The thought amused Jake. He batted the idea around in his mind, teasing out scenarios that could lead to Jake stealing Collin's throne. Jake watched the man in front of him. Collin's power was unnatural and surpassed most by far. It would be suicide to challenge him. No, if there was to be a change in Valefar power this side of Hell, it would be caused by someone other than Jake.

Shifting his feet, Jake pushed the thoughts aside, feeling Collin's hard gaze on his face. When he looked at his master, Collin was less than an inch from him. Clearing his throat, Jake looked directly into Collin's face and reported what he'd learned. "The Martis suspect movement."

Collin arched an eyebrow, refolded his arms, and leaned against the stone wall. They were at the high school where Collin spent much of his time in the auditorium. Acting was something Valefar excelled in. It allowed them a tentative escape from their hellish lives. Jake also dabbled with acting, and knew how dangerous it was to approach Collin here, but the information was too important to waste time. Jake had come looking for him when he realized what was happening.

Collin smiled to himself, as if he couldn't believe it. "And…"

Jake leaned closer, his voice not audible to the human ear, "And it's her—the one who will destroy you and cause the prophecies to fulfill." He smiled at Collin. "She's within reach. The Martis rooted her out. I doubt she even knows what she is yet."

The two separated as footfalls echoed toward them, one step at a time, from the other side of the dark curtain. Collin nodded at Jake and said, "We'll discuss this in detail later." Jake nodded and turned away before he could be seen, and effonated. Collin watched as Jake's form went hazy. It looked like his entire body had heat billowing off of it, like blacktop in the summer sun before he completely disappeared.

Collin leaned against the wall, lost in thought with a soft smile lining his lips. He'd spent the past centuries aware of the prophecy and the girl who would condemn him to death, but until now, he'd never had any idea that he could find her. This single girl would be responsible for the greatest disasters known to her kind, and his. She not only brought about his death, and the annihilation of two races of immortals, but she would also be the sole being responsible for creating the apocalypse. Earth was a stepping stone between

Hell and Heaven. She would be the cause of another angel demon war—a war he didn't want to fight. Wars like that had no winners. Collin's fingers rubbed against his chin. As he was lost in thought the footfalls drew nearer and one of the stage-crew girls rounded the corner.

Collin pushed himself off the wall, and walked past her. The perky girl was clad in pink from head to toe. She smiled at him, opening her mouth to engage him in a conversation in which he had little interest. Not stopping to indulge her, Collin nodded as he passed and said, "Jenna Marie."

CHAPTER TWO

Thoughts of the prophecies consumed Collin. After fumbling his lines beyond belief, he excused himself from rehearsal and walked backstage. Pulling open the metal door that lead to the basement, he walked through and bounced down the steps into the darkness. He could have gone home, but he wanted a chance to think about this on his own. This school was one place where he could be at ease. A new Valefar wouldn't suddenly show up and attack him. Valefar were slow and methodical, certain to thoroughly destroy their victims in every way possible.

Collin rounded the corner at the bottom of the landing. He moved through the darkness with ease and threw his body onto a well-worn couch. Threading his fingers behind his head, he laid there, staring into space thinking about what would happen if he killed the Prophecy One. It couldn't be that easy. There had to be repercussions to destroying her. Would the prophecy just stop? Collin wasn't certain. He'd never seen the prophecies himself. He'd only heard stories of them. The Martis were diligently searching for the girl in the first prophecy painting in the series. And Collin was dying to wrap his fingers around it. Not only would the painting show the face of his assassin, but it would also reveal the ancient words that had been forgotten— words he needed to break his bargain with Kreturus. Collin's chest swelled, and his heart raced at the thought.

No one knew where Collin's power came from. The other Valefar assumed he took the throne to the Upperworld the same way any other Valefar had— through blood and deception. Only the most powerful of Valefar survived. Being ruthless was expected, but Collin's power didn't come from centuries of battles. It came from a bargain—a bargain that cost him more than he realized. Collin pressed his eyes closed, trying to force back the memory. There were few things that truly terrified him, and this was one of them. Try as he might, it was no use. Thinking of the prophecies conjured the memory.

It washed over him in a second and chilled him to the bone. Collin could see himself, ages ago, standing in front of the most powerful demon alive. Kreturus had been trapped in a cave in the Underworld. No one was crazy enough to go looking for him, but Collin did. He moved through the Underworld, killing everything in his path, hell-bent on finding the demon who owned him—and all the other Valefar—so that he could demand his freedom. Collin laughed at the thought. His plan was flawed from the start. There is no such thing as a compromising, level-headed demon. But back then, Collin didn't care. He didn't want the life that had been thrust upon him. He hated the Valefar, though he was one. They were responsible for the pain that he remembered with vivid intensity. He saw it burned onto the back of his eyes every time he blinked - his wife; his child; both ashen faced and laid lifeless on the pyre with flames flickering high into the night sky. The Valefar were to blame. Determination made him reckless, and so Collin found the demon.

The demon's presence was terrifying. He flowed like black ink into every crevice of the cave. The angels contained him in that prison, but the ancient demon shifted his form as needed to make his imprisonment tolerable—until he could find a way to escape. Collin's tenacity didn't falter when the demon's presence wrapped around him like a cloak made of liquid ice. Collin didn't back away, or run screaming as the demon's vapors filled his lungs, as he breathed. Any other man would have cried out in terror. Collin did not. Rage consumed him. The demon's touches only made Collin more irate.

Collin roared, "Return my soul to me! Lift the Valefar curse and let me go free." He looked around in the darkness, expecting to be killed instantly for demanding anything.

But, a low rumble filled the room as Kreturus laughed at him, "You can take all the souls you want."

"No, I can't. I can't take the one soul I need," Collin growled. His jaw locked tight as his hands shook in the darkness clenched into tight fists. There was no way to force the demon to do anything. Collin would have to convince him. He would have to persuade Kreturus into giving him what he wanted. But, Collin had nothing to barter. Kreturus already had his soul.

As if the ancient demon could read his thoughts, the inky blackness seemed to purr. "There is one thing... One thing that I would bargain for."

Shaking, Collin shot upright, and hung his legs over the side of the couch and ended the memory. His heart raced in his chest, beating wildly as he repressed the recollection to the deepest depths of his mind. Leaning forward, he clutched his head between his hands trying to forget. He had given too much. It was a mistake. A mistake that cost him more than he'd already lost.

Startled by the creak of the steps above him, Collin slowly stood and moved through the darkened room trying to see through the metal stairs. The stage lights illuminated the person standing in the doorway until the door clicked shut and darkness cloaked the person. Collin couldn't see who was on the landing above, but heard the creak of each step as the person came closer and closer.

Thinking it must have been an enemy, Collin's body tensed. He moved quickly and pressed himself between two flats that stretched high above him that were leaning, angled against the wall. Moving slowly, he crept behind the canvases. The person moved down the stairs and stopped on the last step, and sat. Collin carefully stepped over props and moved silently through the room. Reaching into his pocket, he pulled out a piece of brimstone. Pressing his finger to the side of the sharp stone, he drew blood and rubbed it against the rock. Instantly, the stone became fluid and changed shape in his hand elongating into a blade, while the section of stone under Collin's grip swelled into a hilt. His grip tightened around the dagger as the stone became hard in his hand. Crouching close to the floor, he approached the staircase from the back. The person sitting there failed to move. They sat utterly motionless breathing in sharp breaths that were too loud for a Valefar, or for someone hunting him. When Collin slid up behind the staircase, he hesitated. Holding his weapon ready to strike, a familiar scent hit his heightened sense of smell. The grip of the blade in his hand loosened as he realized who it was. Collin ran his finger along the blade slicing open his skin. When the blood sank into the black metal, it melted back into a small stone. By the time Collin pressed it into his pocket, his finger had already healed.

He stared at her back for a moment, certain of her identity, and backed away from her. Her lungs expanded filling her body with air as she shook. Collin could hear her sniffle as he moved away, back toward the couch. Pushing his hair out of his face, he looked at her in the darkness one last time. He wished she'd talk to him and tell him what was bothering her enough to sit and cry in the shadows, but he knew she wouldn't.

So, he retreated to the couch and silently sprawled out again. When he reached his hand for the switch behind the couch, he flipped on the lights. With a smile in his voice he said, "Only creepy people sit in the basement in the dark, Ivy."

~VALEFAR VOL. 1 IS ON SALE NOW~

If you love the DEMON KISSED series and can't wait for more, visit with over 43,000 fans on facebook:
Facebook.com/DemonKissed

Or the official website:
DemonKissed.com

OTHER BOOKS BY H.M. WARD

DEMON KISSED

CURSED

TORN

SATAN'S STONE

THE 13th PROPHECY

Coming March 2012

VALEFAR Vol. 1

BANE

Vampire Apocalypse #1

Spring 2012

43741309R00183

Made in the USA
Middletown, DE
17 May 2017